T0130148

THE

SEARCH

IS ON

A Wild Canadian Adventure Continues

BY

Charles L. Wilson

Illustrations by Patricia L. Crum

With a forward by Wayne L. Crum

Order this book online at www.trafford.com
or email orders@trafford.com

Most Trafford titles are also available at major online book retailers.

Printed in Victoria, BC, Canada.

ISBN: 978-1-4269-1812-4 (sc)
ISBN: 978-1-4269-1813-1 (hc)

Library of Congress Control Number: 2009938082

*Our mission is to efficiently provide the world's finest, most comprehensive book publishing
service, enabling every author to experience success. To find out how to publish your book, your
way, and have it available worldwide, visit us online at www.trafford.com*

Trafford rev. 10/26/09

 www.trafford.com

North America & international
toll-free: 1 888 232 4444 (USA & Canada)
phone: 250 383 6864 ✦ fax: 812 355 4082

COVER PICTURE BOOK ONE

Lester and Dora confronted by Old One Ear

REVIEWS FROM BOOK (1)

February 2009

I recently got a chance to read your book and just finished it. It was good. Congratulations, you have done well.

It was as you said. It is fast paced, with no dull moments and it is hard to put down. It is a good family oriented book with Christian values and good moral values all around.

I enjoyed the action adventure of the two youngsters, trying to survive in the wilderness against the elements, the animals and how they often had to work together to save each other.

This book is a pleasant departure from the kind of movies, TV stories, books, and other literature children are exposed to these days.

I like the way the story is told from the interesting prospective of a young boy, and exposes his protective nature of the young girl, which teaches good values and proper behavior for young readers.

It is a pleasant blend of "the Wizard of Oz", Huckleberry Finn", and various themes of man against the elements.

I see it as a great book for both public and private schools to use as extra credit reading and book reporting.

There is a great potential for the book to be used as a class room text on and for developing reading skills, as it will keep the youngster interested and eager to continue reading on and on to the next exciting adventure.

There are good realistic learning examples, for the young people, in the interactions between the central characters and the wild animals that city children have very little opportunity to know about.

If I was still in school I would indeed enjoy reading it to make a book report. I see this story as having the potential to be Walt Disney material for a good clean "action packed adventure movie".

I am hoping you will write more stories and this book will become part of a series.

You did a GREAT job of writing this, Charlie, and I hope to see another one from you.

Thank you for the opportunity and honor to read it.

Dan Brower Walla Walla, Washington U.S.A.)

January 2009

Thank you Charles;

My husband really likes your book and can't wait for the next in the series.

Please send continuing sagas as printed.

I loved it also.

Ellyn Rame Rainier, Oregon (U.S.A.)

January 2009

I really enjoyed your book and I look forward to reading it again, to my kids!

I am also anxious to read the books that follow.

You are very talented and your imagination is amazing.

Any time I see you and Polline (Pat), I will think of Lester and Dora.

Thank you for a copy of your book.

It made a great Christmas gift.

Lori Schmidt "Postmaster" Ferdinand, Idaho (U.S.A.)

February 2009

Thisbookhasbeenwonderfullywrittentocapturetheimagination of our children ages 4 to 17. But we were not prepared for it to do the same to us as parents. As we read A Wild Canadian Adventure it drew our family into the story line so fast that we could not stop reading it. As the title states "Adventure" this is exactly what this book is about, right from the beginning.

I give this book a 5 star rating and encourage everyone to read it. No matter if you are 4 or 80 years old, YOU WILL ENJOY IT!

Kellie A vanHouten Cottonwood, Idaho

(U.S.A.)

March 2009

I like adventure stories, as I go camping a lot in the mountains with my husband and family.

The cover of the book, "A Wild Canadian Adventure, Lost in Canada", caught my eye. I glanced through the book, looking at the pictures. I like doing this before I start reading, and thought that it was just another children's book.

Oh well, I'll read it anyway, but as I read on, I couldn't put the book down. It really had captured my interest. I just had to know what happened next.

This book is not only for children, but for all ages.

I can hardly wait until the next book in the trilogy becomes available.

I really enjoyed it, oh and by the way, I am 77 years young.

Loraine Nelson Priest River, Idaho. (USA)

March 2009

Great children's book. Being a child at heart, at the age of 65 years young, I thoroughly enjoyed the book, A Wild Canadian Adventure. I passed it down to my grandson and he loved it also. Great adventure.

Warren Young Bremerton, Oregon. (USA) Smiling Moon Crafts

May 11th 2009

I thoroughly enjoyed reading A Wild Canadian Adventure-Lost in Canada by Charles L. Wilson. It is a very relaxing and enjoyable read and filled with whimsical adventure. Plan on finishing once you start, because it is impossible to put down. I can hardly wait for the next book in the trilogy.

Karen Coburn Cottonwood, Idaho (U.S.A.)

May 10th 2009

I just finished reading this book. There are many facets to it. It will be enjoyed by children and adults alike. The exciting adventures of two christen children are a pleasure to share. It is action and includes every animal on the North American continent that I can think of. The wonderful animal stories and survival techniques make it a learning experience.

Once you pick this book up you will have a difficult time putting it down. You will want to read it to the end to find out what happens next.

Cathy Bowen Alaska (USA)

May 2009

Hi my name is Christian Smartt. I am Mike Smartts' grandson. I just wanted to tell you that I really liked your book, "A Wild Canadian Adventure." It is the first book in a long time that I have read that I could not put down. It also taught me a

lot about how to survive if I happen to get lost out in the wilderness. I really liked your book and can not wait to read the next one in the trilogy.
Thanks. I am 16 years old.
Chris Smartt.

Caldwell, Idaho. (U.S.A.)

March 2009

It sure was exciting and a real privilege receiving this book. (A Wild Canadian Adventure), from our nephew, Charles L. Wilson. We could hardly put it down. It is sure great to have an author in our family.

We are both looking forward with high anticipation to the next book in the trilogy.

Through out the entire book, the love you have for God and each other shows through.

Mr. and Mrs. Grant Wilson Vancouver, Washington. (USA)

June 14th 2009

I really enjoyed Wild Canadian Adventure book and think you would make a good writer. You are very good at writing books.

Dakotah Rasmussen (9 years old)
Elk, Washington (U.S.A)

June 14th 2009

I really enjoyed all the adventures that Dora and Lester had in this book. I also loved their ever-lasting faith, trust and love for our Lord Jesus Christ. I can't wait for the next books in this

amazing story.

Alicia Dower (13) Spokane Wash. (U.S.A)

August 2009

I am the mother of 4 children, ages 6 through 17. As a Christian, I am constantly looking for wholesome reading material for my kids that they will enjoy.

We read "A Wild Canadian Adventure" together in our home school class and they did not want to stop until we finished the book. I was also caught up in the story, so I read on until the end.

This book is a delight for all ages. It is a, can't put it down, edge of your seat kind of adventure. It is fast paced and very easy to read. The interaction between Dora and Lester is so true to life. You will laugh with them, cry with them, and be overjoyed with their love.

I heartily recommend to any one who enjoys reading to get this book. You will be pleased.

Brenda Copeland (home school teacher) Lewiston Idaho (U.S.A.)

COVER ILLUSTRATION

BY PATRICIA L. CRUM

LESTER AND DORA STANDING IN FRONT OF AN OLD
MINE SHAFT ON COPPER MOUNTAIN

DEDICATIONS

This book is dedicated to my loving family. Without there encouragement along the way, I may never have written this series of books. My wife and children have stood by my side as I reminisced and remembered the important, and sometimes unimportant, things that I have written about in these books.

It has been a very memorable experience for us all as the memories have taken form on these pages. Even as the events, that are illustrated, are fiction, some of them are based on the experiences that my wife, Polline (Pat) Dora Wilson, and I had as children.

For these memories, that my family has encouraged me to remember, and to put down in a series of books, I genuinely thank.

I also dedicate my appreciation to Patricia L Crum, who, with complete dedication on her part, has drawn most all of the illustrations through out these books.

FORWARD
BY WAYNE L. CRUM

Lester and his family had moved to Troy Montana in June of 1952. They lived in an old trailer house that his stepfather had set next to the railroad tracks in Troy. There was a hobo jungle less then a half mile from them.

Watching the hobos ride the rails was one of Lester's favorite pastimes.

Lester had met Dora at the Fourth of July celebration in Troy, and they had become good friends.

Lester was a very adventuresome young man, and loved to do things out of the ordinary. At the beginning of the school year, September 2nd 1952, he had talked Dora into jumping on the old steam train that occasionally passed through Troy.

They found themselves on the train with no way to get off and ended way up in Canada, lost.

They met many wild animals, an old hermit, and unexplainable creatures that many people do not even know exist.

They barely escaped a twelve foot grizzly bear two times, only by the grace of God.

An old hermit took them in and gave them shelter during a forty day snowfall, and taught them how to survive. During this period of time they learned many things that would help them survive the wilderness.

After almost a year, lost in Canada, they mysteriously returned back to September 2nd 1952, with very little memories of what had happened to them.

This is a continuation of, A Wild Canadian Adventure, with Lester and Dora, as told by Lester.

ILLUSTRATIONS
By
Patricia L Crum

TALBLE OF CONTENTS

PREFACE

My family had lived in the little trailer house by the railroad tracks for the last year. My Momma had given birth to a little girl. I now had another little sister. My Momma named her Martha. With the birth of Martha, Momma found the trailer house was way too small, so my stepfather, Leonard, found an old log house, up Iron Creek road, just at the foot of Copper Mountain, about six miles out of Troy. The log house was up for rent and my stepfather was able to rent it. This was great because Dora's family lived just across the creek, less than a quarter mile from the log house. We rode the same bus to school and had become the very best of friends.

Lester and Dora

CHAPTER 1

THE LAST DAY
OF SCHOOL

It was 12:30, Friday afternoon, May 29th 1953, the day before Memorial Day. This was the last day of the school year in Troy Montana. I was just exiting the school, thinking back on how the school year had been.

Dora had passed the third grade and was going into the fourth this coming fall. During the year, I had really missed being with her, and wanted to be in the same room this coming school year. With this thought in my mind, I intentionally failed the fourth grade so that we could be together.

Little did I know, at that time, that the fourth grade class would be so large that we would still be in different class rooms. My failure of the fourth grade was to be a big mistake. Aside from not being in the same class as Dora, the school year had passed very fast.

The old Troy school still looked the same as it had for many years.

I had just exited the front door of the old school house and was standing on the front steps. I had stopped for a moment and was deep in thought about what I wanted to do this summer. I did not see Dora coming toward me. She took me by complete surprise as she grabbed me. I was getting used to this by now as Dora was quite a little bundle of energy and loved spur of the moment decisions, as I did.

I turned around quickly, to make sure that it was she, and saw the excitement on her pretty face. She was breathing hard as if she had been searching for me for some time. I waited patiently until she caught her breath. As she did so she took off again. Looking back over her shoulder she hollered, "well Lester, are you coming or not?" I dutifully started following her wondering what she had in mind.

I had not been able to talk to her this week with all the tests and things that we both had to complete for the school year end.

I caught up to her with some difficulty. She stopped, looked at me and asked, "Aren't you excited?" "Excited about what?" I responded. "Well, about what we are going to do this summer." I did not quite understand, not being a mind reader, but decided to go along with her. She had come up with some interesting things to do this last school year and I figured this might be one of those times.

I remembered when she had talked me into playing a part in the Christmas play. She told me that if I agreed she could get me a leading part and that I would have a lot of fun doing it.

She was true to her word. She had talked the teacher into giving me a leading role. They dressed me up in the costume Dora had chosen for me. I was definitely playing a leading role. Leading the reindeer, that is. I had to play Rudolph red nose and all.

I haven't really forgiven her for that yet.

We were now in back of the school near the playground. Dora sat down on the teeter-totter and motioned for me to sit on the other end. I did so and she excitedly started telling me what she had in mind.

"Lester, I don't know what is happening, but you remember the amulet I always wear around my neck?" I told her yes and asked, "What about it?"

"Well," she said, "it started vibrating yesterday, and will not stop."

"Vibrating?" I asked. "And it won't stop?"

"Lester, are your ears plugged or are you just not listening to me? That's what I said. It's vibrating and won't stop. What do you think it means?"

We had not talked too much about our adventure last fall, but it now started coming back to both of us. We looked at each other and started getting excited as we remembered what had taken place.

I then responded to her last question.

"What if it means we are going to start searching for GeeGee and BeeBee?"

"Do you think so Lester? That would really be wonderful. I can't imagine where we would even start looking."

Thinking back I started remembering what Jocko had said. He had told us that Jonus had taken GeeGee and BeeBee to the surface world. They had run into trouble and only Jonus had returned. Jonus had been shot and died several days later from his wound. The only thing he had been able to tell Jocko and Asheena was that they had been above a little town we call Troy, Montana. Jocko had also explained to us in great detail, that the amulet would be able to lead us to the girls if they were still alive. He told us that the amulet, Dora had around her neck, would vibrate when the time was right.

It had now started vibrating. This made me really excited as I figured now was the time to start searching.

CHAPTER 2
SUMMER BEGINS

Being the last day of school the classes had let out early and the busses would not be arriving until 3:30. It was only 1:00 o'clock, at this time, so we had a couple of hours to kill. Dora mentioned that when the amulet started vibrating, all she could think about was the old cave, we had found, above the school.

When she mentioned this to me I noticed that she was looking at me with a funny expression on her face. I asked her what was wrong. She stood there, for a moment, not saying anything. Then, with surprise in her voice, she said, "Lester, the amulet has quit vibrating." "Wow'" I said, "I bet the amulet was telling you that we are supposed to go to the cave."

We took off on a run. The cave was only about a half a mile above the school so we had plenty of time to go up there and back before the busses would arrive. We had to climb up a steep hill to get to the cave. There was a lot of brush that we had to make our way through so it took us a little longer than what I had figured. After about an hour of climbing we could finally see the opening. It looked the same as it had last summer.

As we entered the opening of the cave we scared a bunch of bats and they came swarming out giving us quite a scare.

We slowly entered the cave. As we did so I heard Dora let out a little giggle. I asked her what was funny about a bunch of bats almost scaring us to death. She looked at me and smiled. "No, that's not the reason I laughed, Lester, the amulet is vibrating again and it tickled." Just as Dora said this I noticed that the crystal, that Jocko had given me, had also started vibrating.

Now the cave was only about thirty feet deep, but it was rather dark as we made our way further in. It was quite hard to see by now and we were wondering what could possibly be here.

Dora was way ahead of me as usual. I hollered at her to be careful and to move a little slower, not wanting her to fall and get hurt.

I had no sooner said this then my crystal started glowing. I pulled the crystal from my neck and it lit up the whole cave. We now could see quite well. We did not know why we were here, but knew that possibly there was something here that we were supposed to find.

We searched for over an hour. It was now about three o'clock and we had to get back down to the school to catch the bus. Just as we were starting to leave a solid ray of red light shot from my crystal. The light was pointing directly at a spot at the far end of the cave.

I made my way carefully to the back of the cave and found a small opening in the back wall. I reached in and felt a small round object. It was stuck and as I tried to remove it from the hole I felt a warm tingling feeling running through my whole body. I slowly maneuvered the object, as best I could, until I was able to partially slide it toward me.

The tingling feeling, that was engulfing my entire being, intensified dramatically. The object felt like it had started vibrating. I withdrew my hand and wiped off the dust that was covering the object. I could not believe my eyes.

It was another solid gold amulet, just like the one Dora had around her neck. Wow, this was really starting to get exciting.

I was deep in thought and had not heard Dora trying to get my attention. She, all of a sudden, grabbed me from behind.

"Lester, we have to get back. The busses will be arriving in just a few minutes and you know how grumpy Joe gets when someone is late for his bus. I don't want to walk home. You can, if you want to, but I'm not going to."

I quickly followed her down the hill. Boy, that girl can really move when she wants to, I thought to myself as I tried to catch up.

The bus had just closed its door and we had to yell to get the Joes attention. He stopped, thank goodness, and we got on.

Joe looked at us with a disgusted look on his face. He then smiled and said. "Well, this being the last day of school I will let this pass this time, but do not be late next year or you will have to walk home."

Joe Sebanforture, the school bus driver. Joe had been our bus driver as long as we could remember. He seemed like a grumpy old man, not allowing any kind of horseplay or the like while on his bus, but we all thought the world of him. I think in his own way he liked most of us.

There were a few kids that were just downright mean to him though and in my mind I don't think he cared much for them, but that was their loss.

As we got onto the bus we found a seat way in back and started talking about what the vibration of the amulet and my crystal lighting up could possibly mean.

Finding this other amulet had really got me excited. It looked identical to the one Dora had around her neck. I just knew it had to belong to either GeeGee or BeeBee.

"Boy," I said, "I think we are in for quite an adventure again this summer," as I started remembering what had taken place last fall and the narrow escapes we had with the huge grizzly bear Old One Ear.

Dora looked at me as I said this. "Yes, I think your right Lester. It seems like everything is coming back into my mind, as if it all had taken place yesterday."

My mom had dinner on the table when I got home. She liked to have dinner early as we lived in an old log house and did not have electricity. The only light we had at night was a couple of old kerosene lanterns and they did not give off very much light.

Leonard had a radio he had pulled from an old wrecked Studebaker pickup. He connected the radio to an old car battery and had it in the house. We spent our evening listening to different stories on the radio.

Leonard liked Fiber McGee and Molly. Mom really enjoyed the detective stories like The Whistler and Dragnet.

Once in a while we would listen to Amos and Andy.

I liked Dean Martin and Jerry Lewis, but my very favorite was The Lone Ranger.

I could sit for hours listening to The Lone Ranger and the adventures he and his side kick, Tonto, had in the old west.

The Lone Ranger was on at eight p.m. Monday night. After the story was over, my mom would tell me it was late and I had better go to bed.

I had a very hard time falling asleep, as all I could think of was what had happened earlier at the old cave. I could not even start to imagine what was about to take place this summer. I just knew Dora and I were about to enter a new world of adventure, and this made me very excited.

I must have finally fallen asleep because the next thing I knew my Mom was trying to wake me up.

"You need to wake up Lester. Its half past seven and the goats are making a lot of noise."

"They need to be milked and staked out. I will have your breakfast ready when you get done with your chores. Here, take these table scraps out to Bozo. And don't forget to give the goats each some water. It's going to get hot today."

CHAPTER 3

GETTING READY

I could hardly wait to go over to Dora's house. I had all my chores to do first and I knew it would take about an hour.

We had 6 goats that I had to milk and take them out to the pasture and stake them out. We did not have a fence around the pasture. I had to drive metal stakes in the ground. I then would tie a twenty-foot chain to the stakes and fasten this chain to each goat so they would not wander off and get eaten by one of the numerous bears that were in the area.

As I was milking Dolly a big bear came through the door. I screamed as loud as I could, shaking the bear up just long enough for me to get out and run toward the house yelling.

The house was over a hundred yards from the barn. My stepfather, Leonard, had heard the commotion and came running with his rifle in hand. The big bear, now knowing that I was not a threat, was chasing me. He was only about a hundred feet behind me. He was closing in on me fast.

I glanced back to see how far away he was from me and my foot hit a big rock and down I went. There I was, all sprawled out on the ground and the bear closing in on me fast. I was so scared I couldn't even move.

The bear was on top of me and all I could see was a huge mouth full of teeth. I just knew I was done for.

Just as I thought I was a goner, Bozo, my dog jumped right on the bears back. The bear reeled around trying to shake Bozo off.

Bozo had his teeth sunk deeply in the bear's neck, hanging on for dear life. The bear reared up on his hind legs bellowing loudly. He started spinning trying to knock Bozo loose. Bozo was hanging on only with his teeth.

With the bear spinning around so viciously, Bozo lost his hold on the bear's neck and fell to the ground. The bear was so mad at Bozo he had totally forgotten about me.

As Bozo hit the ground the bear lunged at him narrowly missing. Bozo took off on a dead run with the bear right behind him. The bear was gaining fast. Bozo had his tail between his legs and running like the wind. He was heading straight toward the goats and they scattered wildly in all directions.

Just as the bear caught up to Bozo I heard a gun go off. Leonard had got into a position to shoot. As he shot the bear stumbled and then veered off heading straight toward the woods.

Bozo had noticed the bear was no longer behind him and regained his courage. He turned around and took off after the bear again.

I thought Leonard had missed the bear completely, because he just kept running.

Bozo was hard on the bears' trail. I tried to call him back, but he would not come. He kept nipping at the bears heals and I was afraid he might get hurt.

The bear was really moving out, but Bozo caught up with him. The next thing that happened really astounded me. Bozo had jumped up and grabbed the bear's tail. It looked like he was trying to stop the bear as he put on the brakes. Bozos' paws were digging into the soft soil raising lots of dust, but the bear did not even slow down.

The bear was running fast, but Bozo hung on for dear life.

As the bear and Bozo disappeared into the woods I heard Leonard call for me to follow him, and we both took off after the bear.

We found the bear, dead, about forty feet into the woods. Bozo was running around the bear barking. When he saw us he jumped up on the bears back and sat up.

It looked to me like he thought he had taken the bear all by himself. He sure looked proud of himself.

I helped my stepfather dress the bear. As we were dressing the bear out Leonard showed me where the bullet had gone. It was a clean shot right through the heart.

I thought to myself, with a sigh of relief, now the goats would be safe. I did not realize that this bear was only one of several that we had to worry about.

As we finished dressing the bear I asked Leonard if I could go over to Dora's house. He said that it was okay with him if my mom said I could. She said it would be okay, but be back before supper.

Dora lived only about a quarter of a mile from our house. I had to cross Iron creek to get there. Dora's father had built a bridge over the creek, and as I was walking across the bridge I heard splashing down in the water. Inquisitive as I was, I crawled down the steep bank and saw several large trout thrashing around in a shallow part of the stream. I thought maybe I could catch them so I rushed over and jumped in. This scared the fish and they tried to get away from me. One of them made a big mistake and went into a shallow eddy.

I jumped in head first, getting my hands under the fish, and scooped him upon to the shore.

Dora's dog, Jerry, had heard all the noise I was making and came down to investigate. He immediately saw the fish and rushed over to get it. I saw what Jerry had in mind so I got to the fish first. Jerry, seeing this, jumped right on my chest knocking me to the ground.

I was able to hold onto my fish and held it away from Jerry. Jerry was on top of me, with his mouth open and fangs showing, growling as loud as he could. He was not a big dog, but I was not about to move and stayed perfectly still.

Dora had seen my predicament and came running to my aid. She called to Jerry, but I think he was having too much fun on my chest and would not get off. Dora had to drag him off. I slowly rose from the ground. Jerry kept snapping his teeth at me. The thought came to me that Jerry did not like me at all.

Just then Dora saw another commotion in the stream. Before I could say anything, she had jumped in the water. "Come on Lester," she screamed, "there's another big fish in here." I saw that she was right and jumped in the water after her. Sure enough, this fish was bigger then the one I had caught. She was scrambling all over in the stream really getting muddy and wet.

"Lester, are you going to help or just stand there gawking at me?" I jumped quickly to her aid. She had the big fish cornered in one side of the creek and I saw that I could grab it from the shore. I reached down to grab the fish, like I had planned, but it flipped its tail and went straight up into the air.

The fish must have gone over three feet straight up. Dora had seen this and immediately grabbed the bottom of her dress and caught the fish.

We took the fish to the shore and were about to congratulate each other when we heard Dora's mother coming down the hill. She looked like she was not really happy. Dora told me that I had better leave right now. I took the advice and left before her mother had got down to where we were standing.

As I was headed toward my house, I could hear Dora's mother raising her voice. I knew that Dora was in trouble. I decided that I could not let Dora take all the blame so I turned around and went back up to Dora's house. Dora and her mother were inside, but had left the door open.

I entered and Dora saw me and motioned for me to leave. I did not. I went over where her mother could see me and said, "Mrs. Garrett. Please do not be mad at Dora. This was my fault and I am sorry." Mrs. Garrett looked at me and said, "I agree with you young man, but Dora knows better then to get her self all dirty like this. Now you go home while I do what has to be done here and then I am coming over to your house and letting your mother know that I am not happy with you."

I learned later that Dora had gotten dressed up in nice clothes, got her hair done up and had on new shoes, getting ready to go to town. I could understand why her mother was so angry. I really felt bad.

Three or four days passed before Dora was able to come over to my house. When she was finally allowed to come over she was dressed in a pair of jeans and a long sleeved shirt.

She mentioned that they ate the fish last night for dinner. She said they were really good and she thought of me as she was eating them. I did not say anything and she let it go.

It was about ten am and it was a beautiful day. There were A few clouds, but no sign of rain. I asked Dora how long she could stay and she told me she could stay until nine o'clock.

The days were long here in Montana and there was daylight in the summer until almost ten pm. We had a long day ahead of us.

Dora was the first to make a suggestion on what we should do. "Why don't we go up on Copper Mountain and check the old mine where the little railroad tracks are?"

I didn't even have to think about it. "Yes," I said, "That really sounds fun. Let's pack a quick lunch and get going. I will grab my hunting knife, a rope and my slingshot and maybe Bozo would like to come with us."

I remembered when I had found Bozo. My mom and I had been out picking huckleberries up by

Spar Lake. We had been picking berries for about an hour when mom heard a noise further up the hill.

She hollered at me that we needed to go, because, she said, she thought she had heard a big old bear above us. I ran over toward her wanting to give her as much protection as I could when we heard a little whine.

Hearing this, I asked my mom if I could investigate. She reluctantly agreed and I made my way through the heavy brush toward the spot where the whine had come from.

I looked around, but could not see anything. I pushed the brush out of the way and all of a sudden this thing exploded in front of me. A big blue grouse flew up right in front of me. I let out a scream, not knowing what it was, and fell backward landing on something soft.

Whatever I had fallen on was growling up a storm. I could not even imagine what was under me. I jumped up, as fast as I could, not wanting to get ate alive.

As I rose up this little ball of fur and big teeth came at me viciously growling. He was chomping his teeth together as if I was going to be its next meal. I jumped back, as fast as I could, tripping over a rock. I fell to the ground hard and the animal was on top of me.

Standing on my chest with mouth wide open and vicious sounds coming from his throat was this little dog.

I was finally able to calm him down, and he started licking me all over as if I was his long lost daddy. I will never forget how I found him. We have been inseparable ever since.

Dora brought me back to reality as she was yelling at me. "Lester, are we going or not?"

Realizing that I had been deep in thought, I looked at her, apologized and started calling Bozo.

I called for Bozo several times, but he did not come. "I guess he is out hunting for a rabbit or something," Dora remarked. I agreed and we got ready to take off. "I am going to let my mom know where we are going," I said.

I told her and she said we needed to be back before it gets dark. I said okay and we packed our lunch and got ourselves ready to climb Copper Mountain.

We had to pass the neighbors chicken coup to get to the foot of Copper. The chickens were raising quite a ruckus and I mentioned to Dora maybe we should check and see what was wrong. She hesitated, but I ran headlong into the coup. I didn't even have a chance to look around when this big animal was all over me knocking me to the ground. Dora had gotten in a position where she could see my dilemma and she took charge.

She ran headlong at the beast screaming at the top of her lungs. Waving her arms like a wild person. The creature, whatever it was, took off running across the field.

Dora had gotten to me at this time and was holding me in her lap, crying. "Lester you have to be all right. Lester please say something, you mean so much to me."

The animal had only knocked the wind out of me and Dora had scared him off before he had hurt me. As I reached up to comfort Dora we heard a shotgun blast. The neighbor had heard the commotion in his chicken coup and had seen the whole thing. As he approached us I heard him holler. "Are you kids okay?"

We told him neither one of us was hurt. "Boy, you kids are sure lucky."

"That was the biggest wolverine I have ever seen."

"Young man, if it hadn't been for this young lady I'm afraid you might not have made it. That was the bravest thing I have ever seen anybody do."

I looked at Dora and she looked at me and we fell into each others arms.

The neighbor, his name was Mr. Davis, invited us in to rest up after our ordeal. Mrs. Davis brought out some cookies and milk and told us her husband had told her what had happened.

"You kids were sure lucky. Wolverines don't generally back down from anything."

We finished the cookies and milk and rested up for a short time. We then decided we might as well continue our trip up Copper Mountain. We thanked Mr. and Mrs. Davis and took off on a run.

CHAPTER 4

OUR SECOND BIG SCARE

There were several ways we could go up on Copper. We decided to take the shortest route. This route was the most hazardous, but it would save us at least two miles of climbing. It was ten thirty now and we figured we could get to the old mine in about two hours or less.

I had taken this trail before and I knew that it wasn't too bad. We had to go over one rocky ridge that had quite a few loose rocks, but with our good leather hiking shoes this should be a breeze.

As we climbed, we were getting more excited with each step. We were now getting closer to the rock ridge.

The grasshoppers were thick and were making their clicking noises. It sounded like music in our ears. I had always enjoyed the sounds of nature.

As we got closer to the ridge we heard an eagle screeching in the sky above us. We looked up and saw the largest golden eagle I had ever seen. He was soaring about one hundred feet above us.

As we watched him he suddenly swooped down toward us.

He came so close; I thought he was going to fly right into us. When he was about three feet away he suddenly veered to the left and went back into the sky.

As we started climbing up the rocky ledge the eagle kept screeching and swooping down toward us. We watched, but did not realize he was trying to tell us something.

As we continued climbing I noticed the rocks on the ledge somehow looked different then they did the last time I was here.

I was about ten feet in front of Dora when all of a sudden the eagle swooped down in front of me again. It startled me so bad that I stopped dead in my tracks.

He landed on a large rock only about five feet from me.

He sat there screeching very loud. I figured there must be something wrong. I very carefully made my around him. He just sat there, on the large rock, watching me.

After making my way to the other side of the rock I noticed the rocks ahead of me looked different somehow.

Something told me to pick up one of the rocks and throw it about ten feet in front of me. I did so and when the rock hit the whole rocky hillside started moving. The eagle took off and Dora and I retreated back down the hill. "Boy," "Dora said "that was a close call." "Yeah it sure was." I said, "Way too close for comfort. We will now have to go the long way around."

It was a little after eleven now and we figured we still had plenty of time to make it up to the old mine and back before nightfall. We followed an old animal trail for about a mile and a half.

We then came upon an old road that was probably used by the miners when they were working the mine. We still had about three more miles to go, but the old road made it a lot easier.

Dora was in front of me looking at everything. There were pieces of quartz that had dropped from the ore wagons, scattered all over the road. She picked one of them up and said. "Look Lester, look at all the gold in this piece." She was right. The gold sparkled brightly in the sun.

We were so interested in the gold that we did not hear something coming up behind us. We both were on our hands and knees looking for more quartz pieces on the road.

All of a sudden something landed right on my back. I knew Dora was next to me so it could not be her. In my mind, with us being way up here in the mountains, I could just imagine a cougar or a big bear attacking me. My whole body felt like jelly and I could not move.

Dora had seen something land on my back and had jumped quickly aside. In her excitement, not knowing what the animal was, she fell backwards into the brush.

She was so entangled in the thick brush there was no way she could get up to help me.

I could feel something warm and wet on the back of my neck. Cold chills enveloped my whole body. I did not know if I had gotten bit and it was blood I felt or what. I couldn't even scream I was so scared.

Dora was finally able to untangle herself from the brush. She saw what was on my back and started laughing.

At this instant the animal, that was on my back, jumped off and started licking the side of my face. "Bozo," I hollered. "You scared me to death. What are you doing here?"

"He must have followed us up the mountain." Dora said. "I can see that," I said, "but I don't understand why you thought it was so funny when he was on my back." Dora again started laughing.

It was half past one by now, but we decided that we still had plenty of time to go on up to the old mine. It was only about another half mile or so. I brushed myself off as best as I could and we continued up the road.

Bozo was way up ahead on the old mining road and was barking at everything he imagined was hiding behind every bush or tree. He had disappeared and the sound of his barking was getting fainter and fainter.

As I was walking along, trying to figure exactly where Bozo was, Dora gently touched my shoulder. I turned to see what she wanted and noticed she had big tears in her beautiful eyes.

"Lester, I am so sorry for laughing at you. When I was able to finally get out of the brush and seeing that it was just Bozo on your back, it looked so funny with you squirming there on the ground I just couldn't contain myself. I would never laugh if you were really in trouble."

I looked at her for a moment. I kind of chuckled. "Yeah, I bet it did look funny. I can just imagine what I looked like, all sprawled out there on the ground with Bozo on my back slobbering all over me with his big wet tongue."

We made eye contact for just a second than we both burst out laughing. It was really funny.

Bozo had gotten so far ahead of us by now that he was completely gone from our sight. We could barely hear his barking way off in the distance. The sound was very faint, but it sounded like he had something treed.

We started running up the old road to see what he had found.

We went around several more corners, but still could not see Bozo.

All of a sudden we noticed that he had quit barking. This made me concerned about him, but figured he could take care of himself.

Bozo was pretty big. He weighed about fifty pounds, and was fast on his feet.

I remembered when he had chased the big old bear that my stepfather had shot and the bear had not been able to even touch him. Bozo had run circles around the bear making him madder and madder.

As we rounded the next corner we saw the old mine in front of us. We could see the big pile of tailings in front of the old mineshaft.

There was an old ore car setting on the tracks just outside the opening to the mine. By the appearance of the ore car it had not been used for many years. The wheels looked like they were totally frozen to the axels from the rust. It must have had a lot of use years gone by.

I remembered pictures I had seen in the encyclopedia at school.

As we were about to go into the mine Dora mentioned that it was now probably after two and maybe we should start back home. I looked at my watch and she was right. It was 2:30.

I looked around for a minute and decided we had plenty of time to eat our lunch. I knew it would not start to get dark until about 9 o'clock and we had no reason to hurry. I mentioned to Dora what I had in mind and she agreed.

"There's a nice spot over by that cedar tree Lester. Let's go over there."

I looked where she was pointing. The tree was big. It must have been over twelve feet to the other side. The tree had grown up right next to a rock wall, and looked very cozy. There was a nice pile of branches lying on the ground. It made a nice soft place for us to sit.

Dora brought out the sandwiches she had been carrying. I had a couple bottles of pop and we sat enjoying our lunch.

As we were eating I heard a noise in the tree above us. Looking up I could not see anything, so I did not mention it, but maybe I should have.

Dora was just finishing her sandwich when I heard another noise above us. This time Dora heard it also. "Lester what's in the tree above us? Maybe we better move." I agreed, but before we could even get up something fell out of the tree landing right on top of Dora's head. She let out a blood curdling scream, sending chills up and down my spine.

Dora had gotten up and was flailing her arms wildly, trying to get away from whatever it was on her head. I had seen what it was and was trying to get close enough so that I could pull the animal off. With her arms moving around so wildly I was unable to get a hold on the little beast.

Dora was now out in the open still pulling and yanking at the little animal and screaming at the top of her lungs.

I finally was able to get close enough to her and tried to pull it off her neck, but could not. It was hanging on for dear life. I think it was more scared then Dora.

As I was able to get closer to Dora, I got my hands under the little fellow and gently tugged.

Dora had completely worn herself out by now and was not screaming quite as loud. The little guy let go and I had him in my arms. He just laid there trembling.

Dora was so tired from all the effort she had expelled, that she fell to the ground and just laid there. I put the little animal on the ground and rushed over to help her. She was lying very still. I hugged her and she fell into my arms crying. I comforted her as best I could. After a few minutes she settled down.

"What was that? Is it gone? Did you see it Lester? Am I okay? Will it come back?"

Before I could answer she had jumped up and started looking around. She spotted the little animal immediately. "Is that what was on me?"

I nodded yes. She looked at me with wide eyes and started laughing and crying at the same time, as she saw what it was. She walked over and picked the little guy up. It cuddled right into her arms and nuzzled its little nose on her neck. It was a little red fox.

"Do you think I can keep it Lester?" "No." I said. "His mother is probably not to far away and he still needs her. You better put him down." Dora let out a whine, but knew I was right.

She sat the little fox on the ground and he immediately scooted back toward the cedar tree. As we watched him he ran behind the tree and up a rock ledge.

Up about ten feet was a small cave. At the mouth of the cave we could see three more little fox pups. Momma fox was no where in sight.

I figured she was probably out hunting for her little family.

The cedar tree had grown in such a manner that one of the branches had extended itself into the mouth of the cave. The little fox must have made his way along the branch and then lost his footing, falling on Dora. "You saved his life Dora. He fell on you and not the ground. He could have really been hurt if he had hit the ground."

Dora looked at me with a big beautiful smile on her pretty face. "Yes, I did. Didn't I?" She took off down the hill.

I called for Bozo, but he did not come. I knew he could find his own way home so I took off at a dead run. Dora was in the lead and yelled over her shoulder. "Bet I can get home before you Lester." She took off like a shot. Boy I thought, as she disappeared from my sight, that girl can run.

I did my best, but there was no way I could catch her and there was no way she was going to let me. She was very competitive and always liked being first. This was okay with me.

Dora was at my house waiting for me. "What took you so long Lester?" She smiled as she asked this. Before I could answer, she took off again. "See you tomorrow around seven Lester. Bye."

Next morning I got up about six, did all my chores and was about to eat breakfast, when Dora appeared outside the back door. She looked real cute. She had her hair done up in pigtails with a red bandana around her neck. She had on a pair of Levis with red suspenders. Her shirt was long sleeved with blue stripes. High topped shoes were on her feet.

She was ready for climbing up the mountain.

Much to my dismay Jerry was with her. That dog hated me with a passion and I had a very hard time liking him. I did not want to hurt Dora's feelings so I didn't say anything.

I invited Dora to come in as I was still getting my things together for the climb up Copper. She told my mom hi as I finished getting ready.

I decided to take my backpack and a few things I thought we might need in the old mine. I grabbed a rope, flashlight, matches, hunting knife, slingshot, and a bag of marbles.

As I passed through the kitchen to go outside, mom grabbed me and gave me a bag of sandwiches. "You might like this later," she said. I thanked her, found Dora waiting outside and was about to tell her I was ready when all of a sudden Jerry attacked me from behind.

He had a death hold on my pant leg. Dora grabbed him and told him to be good. Yeah right, be good Jerry, I thought to myself, as he looked at me suspiciously, uttering this deep menacing growl way down in his throat. There was no way in my mind I could visualize Jerry being good.

I thought about how, when I visited Dora at her house for the first time, Jerry had greeted me. When Dora had got off the school bus she had invited me to come over to her house to meet her parents. She had not mentioned that she had a little black demon in the form of a dog that hated everything.

Jerry spotted me immediately as I crossed the bridge over Iron Creek. He hurriedly came out to greet me. Little did I know what kind of disposition he would have. I reached down to pet the cute little guy when he exploded.

He jumped up at me and landed right on my chest, knocking me to the ground. He had me at his mercy. I moved my head from side to side, trying to avoid his fowl breath. As I did so his fangs stayed right in front of my face.

Dora, seeing what had taken place and also hearing the noise I was making came to my rescue. Grabbing Jerry, she pulled him off me.

I have stayed away from Jerry as much as possible ever since that day. Now he was going with us up Copper. How nice. I could just imagine how much fun Jerry was going to have.

We took the long way up Copper and experienced no problems. We had not seen Bozo since we left the old mine yesterday and I was thinking about him and where he could possibly be. I could just imagine him finding all kinds of things in the mine that he could chase and bark at. I knew he could take care of himself, but I was still a little concerned.

CHAPTER 5

EXPLORING THE OLD MINE

As we approached the mine, we saw something moving just inside the opening. We could not tell what it was, but we could see that it was big. The animal was running back and forth as if it was searching for something.

As we got closer to the front of the old mine we could see it was Bozo. He saw us approaching and came out all happy to see us. He jumped on me almost knocking me to the ground.

I pet him and he seemed satisfied that I still loved him, and took off back into the mine.

Jerry was right behind him, barking and yapping at the top of his lungs, trying to keep up with Bozo.

There was a lot of old mining equipment lying around. The ore cars were all rusty and looked like they had not been used for years.

The rails, that the ore cars were sitting on, went from the top of the tailing pile clear back into the old mine shaft as far as we could see.

We could hear Bozo and Jerry again way deep in the mineshaft. The sound was amplified as it reverberated from the walls of the mineshaft tunnel.

They must have thought they owned the whole mine and that they were chasing out any and all possible intruders that might be in their mine.

Several big bats flew out of the mine tunnel and swooped down toward us. We both dodged, but the bats seemed determined to get us.

Dora picked up a big club and stood there like a baseball player ready to hit a home run. Much to my surprise as one of the big bats came at her she swung and connected.

That old bat didn't even know what hit him. He went sailing out of sight. Boy, I thought to myself, you can be on my team any time.

We went over to check the bat out. We spread the wings out and they stretched out over two feet wide from tip to tip. Claws were on the tips of the wings and they sure looked vicious. They were over two inches long. His mouth was full of fangs. I could just imagine how much damage he could do if he had gotten hold of one of us.

He was really ugly. I thought about how he looked like a huge mouse with wings and fangs. I had never seen a bat this big and was wondering if there were any more in the old mine.

On the far side of the mine we noticed an old steam donkey.

As we were looking at the old steam donkey we again heard Bozo and Jerry barking way down deep in the old mine. Thinking that they might possibly run into a skunk or something worse we decided that maybe we should go in after them and see what all the commotion was all about.

As we entered the old mineshaft we could see that the ore car tracks were continuing in as far as we could see.

Patricia A[...]

We continued following the tracks. As they turned several bends in the mineshaft we felt like we going through a long tunnel. It was starting to get darker and we were wondering if we should turn back when all of a sudden my crystal started vibrating.

I pulled the crystal from my neck and it started glowing with a very bright white light. It was glowing so bright that it lit up the whole tunnel all around us. This was nice as we were able to continue.

We were now able to see that the old mine tunnel was supported by large logs placed every twelve feet or so along the sides. All the supports looked to be in pretty good condition so we were not afraid of the roof caving in on us.

We could still hear Bozo barking somewhere way ahead of us. Dora mentioned that his barking seemed never ending and asked me if he ever shut up.

I told her that I could remember sometime back, when he was a pup, there was one instance that he was quite.

I had woke up early that morning and caught him in bed asleep, but that was the only time I could remember he was not making some kind of noise.

Just then something strange happened. Dora and I both listened intently and we could not hear anything at all. There was no sound anywhere. We both started getting very nervous as we could not figure out what was wrong.

There was a deathly silence filling the entire mine tunnel. We both felt like we had been put in an airtight vacuum of some sort.

As we were wondering about the silence Jerry appeared out of the darkness. He came running toward us at full speed. When he was about six feet from us he made a big leap right into Dora's arms. He laid there trembling. I knew there was something terribly wrong because he didn't even growl at me as he passed.

From out of nowhere Bozo came running toward us. He had his tail between his legs like he had seen a ghost or worse yet maybe a monster or something. He got between Dora and me and just stood there shaking. I could not figure out what had scared him so bad, but it must be something really big.

Bozo was the kind of dog that would not back down from anything and yet here he was, scared to death. Wow, I thought to myself, this is really starting to shake me up.

Even though this really shook me up I knew we had to continue into the old mine tunnel. My crystal had started vibrating stronger and I knew in my heart we had to go on no matter what.

As we continued through the mine tunnel we could hear somewhere deep in side some kind of humming sound. The humming had somewhat of a musical tone to it and was very pleasant to our ears.

By now we must have been at least fifty feet or more inside the tunnel. Dora softly mentioned maybe we should turn back.

Just as she said this the light that was glowing from my crystal changed to a beautiful blue color. The light again lit up the whole tunnel and we could see way back in.

There were quite a few large shiny objects on the walls of the tunnel. The objects looked like they were pure gold.

We decided, with the crystal changing colors, we were supposed to go deeper into the tunnel. As we continued the humming sound was getting louder and louder. I could not imagine what the sound was, but it sure sounded strange and different then before.

We went around several more corners and my crystal started vibrating stronger.

Bozo was still between us and Dora was still carrying Jerry. Looking at Jerry I thought to myself, as mean and ferocious that he is toward me, he sure was a big baby. Every once in a while he would let out a little whine.

Something earlier must have really shaken him up. I have never seen him so meek and scared.

My crystal was really vibrating now. As we went around the next corner Dora suddenly grabbed my arm hard. "Lester." she said, "Look at that light coming out of the ground." There in front of us was a big hole in the floor. Shining from the hole was the brightest green light I had ever seen.

As we approached the hole the blue light that was shining from my crystal changed to the same color green as was shining from the hole.

I knew this had to have some meaning, but could not understand what it meant.

At this point the humming sound changed pitch. The tone was so high that it was hurting our ears. Bozo did not like it either and was about to take off toward the entrance. Just then the humming stopped.

The floor of the mine tunnel started trembling. I thought sure an earthquake had started. The walls looked like they were, like, in some kind of a warp. We felt like we were caught in a whirlwind.

Jerry jumped out of Dora's arms landing right on top of Bozo. Both dogs then took off heading straight toward the mine entrance.

All of a sudden we were both picked up off the ground. Some force had us in its grasp and we were spinning around in the air. The lights all went out and we found ourselves in total darkness.

Dora reached out grabbing me hard, almost squeezing the air right out of me. We were both scared, not knowing what was happening. What were we going to do?

CHAPTER 6

THE CAVE

As we were spinning, or were we falling? I could not tell, Dora held on to me tightly. I felt like a big old grizzly bear had me in its clutches, making me feel like I was about to be squeezed to death.

I heard a noise that was unbearable. I cannot explain what it sounded like, but it was very deep and made my whole inner being feel like I was going to vibrate apart.

The sound made me have cold chills all over my entire body. It felt like we were being thrown through time and space. What was happening?

All of a sudden all was quite. We had stopped spinning and it felt like we had landed on something soft.

My crystal, had again, started vibrating, and a soft blue light was starting to shine from it.

As the light slowly got brighter I noticed we were in a large cavern of some sort. Dora had loosened her bear hug on me and I felt like I could breathe again.

Just then I remembered Bozo and Jerry. Where were they? The last time I saw them we were standing on the floor of the old mine and the floor had started trembling.

Dora and I searched everywhere. They were nowhere to be found. We both called, but there was no answer. They had just disappeared.

As the hours passed we continued our search, covering every nook and cranny of the old mine tunnel. Bozo and Jerry were gone.

At the far end of the cavern was a very large boulder. Looking closer we were able to see that we could slip behind the boulder, and found an opening just large enough for us to squeeze through.

In front of us was a horizontal shaft. The shaft looked to be about six feet high and we were able to walk upright.

The floor of the shaft was smooth and the going was easy. We noticed the shaft was getting bigger. There was a faint light in front of us. Wondering what the light was, we both got excited and started running. As if by magic we found ourselves in a very large room.

The walls were all solid rock with stalactites hanging all around. One of the stalactites was hanging all the way to a mound on the floor. There was a small ledge at the top of the walls, running all the way around the room. The room was circular and stretched about fifty feet across.

There was a high ceiling and some kind of phosphorescent rocks were glowing brightly. They lit up the entire room with a strange sort of white light.

The light kind of gave me an eerie feeling as it was shimmering in a very unusual manner. It felt like it was vibrating and the vibration seemed to be entering my entire body. It felt funny, but did not hurt. I guess it was kind of pleasant.

Looking around we noticed two triangular shaped mounds in the center of the room on the floor.

As we got closer we could see that the mounds appeared to have been formed from the water dripping from the ceiling. I remembered from school that these were stalagmites.

The mounds were about two feet high. On top of each tiny mound was a beautiful red stone of some sort. The stones looked like large rubies.

The inside corner of each mound was about one foot from the corner of the next mound.

We were able to see a rock wall in back of the mounds. In the middle of the rock wall was a cave. The cave was in perfect alignment with the red stones on top of the two of the mounds.

Dora reached out and touched my shoulder. "Lester, the amulet I found in the cave in Canada is starting to vibrate. What do you think it means, Lester?" "I don't know, but I hear some kind of sound. I think it's coming from the cave over there."

At that moment we both heard something rushing up behind us. It was not light enough for us to see what was coming toward us, but whatever it was it was sure making a lot of noise.

I grabbed Dora's arm and started running toward the mounds. In my haste I tripped over a rock and landed right smack dab between the two mounds. As I tripped I had let go of Dora and she fell on the floor beside one of the mounds.

She was lying very still. She had hit her head on a large rock. I tried to get up to go help her, but I could not move. My whole body felt like it was paralyzed.

I hollered at Dora several times, but she did not answer.

I tried several more times to get up, but could not. Just then I noticed some movement at the far side of the cavern. Bozo, all of a sudden, came into view, and rushed over towards me.

As he got to close to the mounds he yelped and stopped, as if he had hit a brick wall. He looked at me, lying there and tried to come toward me again. One more time he let out a yelp and stopped. Bozo could not get closer then three feet from the mounds. I noticed that the red stones on top of the mounds were glowing brightly.

I did not know what to do. Dora was on the floor unconscious and I could not move. Bozo could not get to me because of some kind of invisible barrier surrounding the mounds. "I prayed, *"Lord, what am I going to do? Please let Dora be okay."*

Just then I heard a sound kind of like something being dragged. A very bright light appeared in the opening of the cave. Bozo started barking wildly, as if he had seen something really scary. I knew now we would not make it home before dark and our parents would be very worried. At that moment, everything went completely black.

"Lester, I'll see you tomorrow. If mom will let me I will be here about seven so we can get an early start. Come on Jerry, let's go home."

"Tomorrow, early start, what, where am I. What's going on? Were home? Dora, Dora, what's happening? Bozo, get down. Why are you jumping on me? What's wrong with you?"

The next thing I heard was my mom. "Lester, Lester, come in and get ready to eat. Your food is going to get cold if you don't get in here right now."

I don't understand what's happening, but we're safe, back home and okay. What's going on? "Bozo I told you to get down!"

Something really strange is going on. How could we be here at home? The last thing I remember I was stuck between the two mounds and Dora was lying on the ground unconscious.

I did not learn until much later what had taken place.

"Lester, get in here right now." "I'm coming Mom."

I knew we had to get back to that cave somehow, someway. I knew in my heart we must be very close to finding GeeGee and BeeBee.

CHAPTER 7

GEEGEE FINDS US

I slowly opened my eyes and tried to raise my self up, but could not seem to move a muscle. It felt like I had a heavy weight holding me down. It was totally dark, but I could make out some sort of light about forty feet away.

The light was bluish in color and there was some kind of movement just beyond. A deep reverberating hum filled the air.

I tried to remember what had happened and where I could possibly be. Everything was a blank in my mind and all I could remember was that Dora was with me. Dora, wow, yes, Dora. Where is she? I started yelling her name as loud as I could. "Dora, Dora." I kept yelling. There was no answer.

I again tried to get up and was able to move just a little. It seems like the light was now getting brighter. Just then I heard a noise. It sounded like people, but I could see no one.

The next moment a bright light lit up the entire area. I was in a large room of some sort. Looking around the room, there were several large boulders and something that appeared to be sand on the floor. The sand was a very beautiful pinkish color. Small shiny things were scattered everywhere.

I was lying on something that was very soft and comfortable. Over in one corner of the room was a large round object on the rock wall. Whatever the object was, it had a shimmering light emanating from it. It somewhat looked like a waterfall, but the water looked like it was flowing in all directions at the same time, but there was no water. It was very beautiful.

I again tried to move and knocked something to the floor, making a loud racket. I tried to get up, but could not. It seemed like I was tied down and I could not figure out why.

All of a sudden two figures appeared as if they had materialized right out of the wall. They literally appeared out of nowhere.

Not being able to see very well, I could not tell what they were. One of them was quite large and was walking with a real bad limp. The other figure was quite a bit smaller. Wow, what's going on? I again tried to get up, but could not.

The figures started coming toward me. They seemed to be deep in conversation. I was wondering who or what they were when the smaller one reached down and gently touched my head.

At that moment the light, all of a sudden, got bright and I was able to see what it was.

It was Dora and beside her was a large individual with hair all over its body.

Dora grabbed my hand and gently rubbed my head with her hand. "Lester, look who found us. Look Lester, GeeGee found us. She has been taking care of us. She nursed me back to health, and you have a poultice on you that will make you well. GeeGee says you will be okay in just a couple of hours or so."

I rose up a little bit and was able to mumble a few words.

"How-how did we get back here Dora?" I asked in complete wonderment. "Did you say GeeGee? How do you know she is GeeGee?"

"She told me that she was watching us as we entered the cavern where the tiny mounds are. She saw us both fall and knew we needed help. She had seen bozo running toward us, barking. Thinking that he meant us harm, she chased him away."

"I was only knocked out and came to as she picked me up. Seeing you were injured worse than I was, she started tending you."

"When I saw her I thought that she was Madeena. 'Madeena?' I asked. She turned and looked at me with a startled look on her face. 'No, my name is GeeGee' she said. At that moment we heard you trying to move and rushed down to help you."

GeeGee took this moment to interrupt and asked, "What are you children doing here, and how do you know my mothers name?"

Before either one of us could answer Bozo and Jerry came into the cavern, barking at the top of their lungs. GeeGee, as she saw them rushing madly toward us, put herself between them and us.

Dora grabbed GeeGee's arm and explained that they were our dogs and they would not hurt any of us. GeeGee relaxed and sat back down. Both dogs jumped on us and acted like they had not seen us for days.

As Bozo and Jerry settled down, all kinds of questions started filling my mind. I remembered what Jocko had told us. Thinking about this I asked GeeGee what had happened to her and BeeBee. And how can we be here in this cavern, and we were just home and now we are here.

"Just one question at a time young man. All things in nature need to be in perfect harmony to be able to react properly to their surroundings. One of the many gifts our creator gave us is to be able to harmonize to our surroundings."

"Harmonize? What does harmonize mean GeeGee?" asked Dora.

"Harmonize means that we can, with the proper vibration-al state of our minds and body, be in tune with our surroundings. All things in nature vibrate. If you can achieve control of your vibration-al state most anything can be done. Even the healing of most diseases can be accomplished."

CHAPTER 8
GEEGEE'S STORY

GeeGee looked at me for a moment. She seemed to realize that Dora and I might be able to help her rescue BeeBee. She started telling us what had happened to them when she and BeeBee got separated from their Uncle Jonus.

"We had just reached the surface world and everything was going along fine when all of a sudden Uncle Jonus fell to the ground. Then we heard a loud explosion. We saw four humans running toward us. They were yelling at the top of their lungs. Each man had a rifle and I just knew that Uncle Jonus had been shot."

"Uncle Jonus told us to run and not look back. That was the last we saw of Uncle Jonus. BeeBee and I wandered around for days, trying to get back to the opening to our world. The hunters just kept after us and we traveled further and further into the forest."

"We came upon a cave above one of your little towns."

"It looked as if might make a good hiding place. I mentioned this to BeeBee and she agreed."

"BeeBee and I entered the cave."

"We found some old branches and covered the opening so that it could not be seen. It was still quite early in the day, so we decided to stay in the cave until nightfall. We thought, maybe, we could sneak past the men with the darkness of night and get back to the opening to our world."

"Just as we were starting to make ourselves comfortable we heard the men outside the cave opening. We were able to hear the men talking."

"Three of them were beating the brush with big sticks and shooting their guns into the sky. The other man was looking right at the opening to the cave. He came closer to the cave and started pulling the brush away. He let out a loud yell to the other men and they came running."

"BeeBee and I hurried back as far as we could possibly go into the cave. We found an opening just large enough for both of us to fit and we squeezed in as far as we could."

"There were several large boulders lying on the floor of the cave and we were able to use them to close the opening to our hiding spot. They did not have any form of light so we hoped they could not see us."

"Squeezed together in the tight hole was very hard and we were so thirsty that I was afraid we would die right there. The men searched for a few more hours before they finally gave up."

"After they left I told BeeBee we had better stay put for several more hours to be safe. We finally felt it would be safe so we nervously left the cave. In my nervous state I had not felt my amulet being ripped from my neck and didn't know where I had lost it."

"By this time, what with all the excitement, we had wandered so far from where we had last seen Uncle Jonus , that neither one of us knew which way to go. We were hoping, against all odds, that maybe he had not been hurt to bad and that he would find us."

At this point GeeGee stopped and sobbed ever so slightly. She then continued.

"We finally found a small stream and followed it. The water in the stream was flowing faster and faster and there was a loud roaring sound somewhere in front of us. As we continued we found where all the noise was coming from. It was a big water fall."

"We made our way down below the falls and looked back."

"The falls were beautiful. There was a large bull elk standing below the falls looking at us. He was sure beautiful."

"We stood and watched the majestic animal for a long time."

"We were just about to continue on when BeeBee grabbed my arm. She motioned to the other side of the stream. I looked and saw a big hulk of a man. He had a long grey beard and long grey hair that flowed way down his back. He was carrying a big gun."

"As we watched in horror the man raised the gun. We heard a loud explosion. This was the exact sound we had heard when Uncle Jonus had fallen to the ground. The sound reverberated around on the canyon walls. The poor elk went down hard on the ground and the man started running toward him."

"BeeBee screamed and ran at the man with her arms flailing wildly. I jumped up and tried to stop her. The man saw her coming, raised his gun and shot. He missed her, but I was right behind her and the bullet hit me in the hip."

"By this time BeeBee was right on top of the man. He slammed the stock end of his gun on her head. BeeBee went down and did not move. He then raised his gun at me again and fired. He missed and I had to run into the forest and hide."

"I waited around and hid in the forest for a few hours as the man dressed out the elk. He finished dressing the elk and threw it high in a tree. I figured he was going to come back for it later."

"BeeBee was still unconscious. The man was so powerful that he was able to pick BeeBee up, throw her over his shoulder, and took off into the woods. I was hurting so bad by this time, that I could not follow. I hoped that I would be able to follow his tracks later and rescue BeeBee."

"I was still by the falls the following morning and was woke up by harsh laughter. As I rose up I was able to see the big man was back. He was retrieving the elk from the tree. He threw the big animal over his shoulder and took off through the woods. I was feeling better so I was able to follow him."

"We must have walked for several hours. By this time, my leg was really starting to bleed again and I had to stop. The man continued and I lost sight of him at the bottom of Grouse Mountain. That was the last time I saw BeeBee."

GeeGee stopped at this point and then softly said more to herself then aloud. "If only I had my amulet." GeeGee stopped and started crying softly.

As I heard GeeGee say this I happened to remember the amulet that Dora and I had found above the school in the old cave. Before I could say anything Dora had pulled her amulet from around her neck. "GeeGee, I have this amulet that I found in Canada when Lester got me lost."

GeeGee, hearing what Dora said, turned quickly around. She was wide eyed and very excited. "Can I see that?" she asked.

Dora handed the amulet to GeeGee and GeeGee immediately turned it over to look at the back.

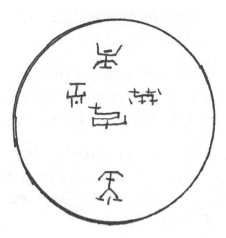

All of a sudden she burst out with a voice full of excitement. "Where did you get this?" she asked.

Dora, seeing how excited GeeGee was, saw the opportunity to tell her how we had gotten lost in the Canadian wilderness. She explained to GeeGee how I had got her lost and how we had found the amulet by accident in the old cave.

"Lester made me walk in this creek and it was very cold. I saw this old cave on the left side of the creek and I told Lester we should go in the cave to get warm. It was nice inside the cave so we started looking around. I saw something shiny beside a large rock. When I pulled on it this amulet was on the other end."

GeeGee interrupted Dora at this point. "This amulet belongs to my Uncle Jonus. You see the symbol on the back? The symbol, in the center of the amulet, tells to whom the amulet belongs. They have very strong power for each one of us, but the amulet only works for its owner or in conjunction with other amulets."

"We are each presented with our amulet at birth and we carry it with us at all times. He would never have left it behind without a cause."

"Did you see my Uncle Jonus?" Dora turned and looked at me as if she did not know what to say. I kind of stammered as I told GeeGee that we had not seen her Uncle Jonus.

Thinking back on what Jocko had said about finding Jonus and him dying, we were both concerned that if we said anything we would hurt GeeGee's feelings.

GeeGee looked at us and I knew she had seen our nervousness. I noticed tears forming in her eyes. Before anything else could be said, she extended her arms motioning for us to come to her and she gave us a big hug.

Right at that moment my crystal started vibrating so hard that I forgot about the amulet I had around my neck. The crystal was vibrating so violently that I had to remove it from my neck. As I removed it the crystal levitated out of my hand. It floated over to GeeGee. GeeGee reached out and caught it.

"You have been to my world and talked to my Grand father Jocko!" She exclaimed. Just then the crystal started glowing and we all were silent. GeeGee put the crystal on the floor. As she did so a ray of white light came from the crystal in the form of a fan.

As we watched, a holographic form of Jocko appeared. He began talking.

"GeeGee, Lester and Dora have been in our world as you have already realized. Dora has your Uncle Jonus's amulet. If you take your amulet, your cousin's amulet, your Uncle Jonus's amulet, and this crystal, you will be able to open a portal between our world and the surface world."

"When all the amulets are together, this crystal will once more activate and I will tell you what needs to be done." The light from the crystal slowly dispersed, and the hologram disappeared.

GeeGee reached down and picked up the crystal and handed it back to me. "Guard this well Lester. We might need it sometime in the future, if I can find my amulet."

As GeeGee handed the crystal back to me, I reached out with my left hand to accept it and slipped into my pocket.

With my right hand I pulled the amulet that Dora and I had found in the cave above the school, from my neck. I reached out and placed it in GeeGee's hand. She took it, saw that it was an amulet, and as she turned it over, she started crying. "Lester," she sobbed, "where did you find my amulet?"

I started to tell her where we had found the amulet, when Dora jumped in. "We were exploring the old cave above the school house when Lester's crystal shot out a bright red light. The light pointed at this hole in the wall of the cave. Reaching in Lester found the amulet. I told him that he better keep it safe because it was just like the one that I had found when we were lost in Canada."

GeeGee, as if not hearing a word Dora had said, was looking at the back of the amulet. As she was doing this she was pressing the different symbols on the back.

All of a sudden a very bright beam of red light shot out from the center symbol on the back of the amulet. The light seemed to have a mind of its own as it sought out and saturated GeeGee's wounded leg. I could hear a high frequency hum which was very pleasant to my ears.

As we watched, in absolute wonder, the bullet came to the surface and fell to the floor. As the piece of lead hit the floor another beam of blue light shot from the amulet covering the wound with a bright vibrating glow. The wound suddenly disappeared as if had never been there.

Seeing what had just happened, Dora could not contain herself. "How did you do that GeeGee? That's not possible."

GeeGee smiled at Dora as she started explaining what had just happened. "All things that exist vibrate at their own rate. Nothing can exist without a state of vibration. When I was born my amulet was created, as are amulets for all Hgiahs. Our amulets are set to the same frequency as our internal system."

"When something happens to our body, in any way, including injury, our amulets have the power to readjust the frequency of our system back to its original state. When this is done, any problems are corrected, short of death."

At this point I could not contain myself. "You're saying that all diseases can be healed using vibration at the right frequencies?" GeeGee smiled. "Yes Lester, that is right."

GeeGee raised her head, looked at us with a big smile and said. "Thank you both so much. I thought I would never see my amulet again."

"You have restored my faith that I might be able to find BeeBee." Saying this she again raised her amulet and started pressing several of the symbols on the back. As she did this she waved it over me. I looked at her in amazement.

My whole body felt wonderful. The pain, that had been enveloping my whole body, was gone. "What happened?" I asked. "You have been totally healed." She said. "Now we need to go."

CHAPTER 9

The Bull Moose Encounter

As GeeGee said this she walked over to the mounds. She was holding her amulet in front of her, pressing several of the symbols on the back.

As she approached the mounds the jewels on top of each one started glowing. "Lester, Dora, you need to get right in the center of the mounds, now!"

Without hesitation I grabbed Dora, before she could ask why, and jumped right in the center. GeeGee was right behind us. The next instant we were standing on the shore of a big beautiful lake.

"What just happened, GeeGee?" I asked. GeeGee looked at me and smiled. "You and Dora experienced the power of the mounds earlier." I looked at GeeGee with a question on my face. GeeGee seen this and continued.

"When you fell into the center of the mounds and got hurt, you were thinking how you and Dora needed to return home before dark. The powers of the mounds are generated by deep emotional thought. As you were thinking of returning home the power generated by your thought was turned into reality, or so you imagined. You and Dora were instantly returned home."

"But it seemed like when I woke up the next morning I was still in the cavern and I heard you and Dora talking. I do not understand GeeGee."

"What you experienced, Lester, was something you humans do not understand. The illusion you experienced was what you might call a dimensional rift."

"Dimensional what?" Dora asked.

"Dimensional rift. This, as some of your scientists have discovered, is where a parallel world exists in a different dimension. You and Lester are home in the parallel dimension and yet you are still here. Your parents will now not be worried about you."

This did not make any sense to me whatsoever. Parallel dimension? Dimensional rift? Dora and I are home, yet we are still here? Wow! Two places at the same time.

I was deep in thought pondering on this and did not see GeeGee trying to get my attention. Dora grabbed my arm and pulled me around hard. She pointed at GeeGee.

GeeGee was motioning for to us to get down. She told us to get into the low bushes and stay there until she returned. Upon saying this, she took off around the lake.

We stayed under the bushes, for several hours, wondering when GeeGee would return. We were really starting to get worried when we heard something coming toward us. The brush was thick and besides that, it was dark under the bushes, and we could not see a thing.

There was a loud splash as if something huge had jumped in the water. Deep grunting followed the splash. We were only about twenty feet from the water, but could not see a thing.

The splashing was getting louder by the second and we were really getting scared. Dora grabbed my arm. "What are we going to do?" she whimpered.

Before I could think of an answer a loud bellow permeated the forest. Whatever it was out there sounded like it was coming right toward us.

There was no place for us to go. I grabbed Dora and pulled her to the ground. She started to say something and I put my hand over her mouth. I knew we had to be still and not make a sound.

The creature was getting very close by now and I just knew he would smell us.

At that exact moment something picked us both up and it felt like we flying through the air.

Just then GeeGee's voice sounded in my ears. "It's okay Lester. I have you both now. Hold on, it's a bull moose and he's really mad. I have to move fast so do not be afraid."

GeeGee could really run, but the Bull Moose was gaining on us fast.

I was able to sneak a peek back and the moose was less then ten feet from us. I was about to mention this to GeeGee when all of a sudden we were airborne.

GeeGee had just jumped over a cliff. We landed and GeeGee stopped and put us both down.

Wow, what a ride. I looked back and saw that the cliff was more than forty feet to the top. What a jump!

The moose was at the top of the cliff, and he really looked mad. "Boy that was exciting." Dora exclaimed. "But let's not do it again!"

As GeeGee had been moving so fast running away from the moose, we found ourselves way below the lake by a large stream. Leafy trees were on the shores and the entire area was beautiful. GeeGee, seeing that Dora and I looked like we were wore out, decided we should spend the night here.

We found a nice area under the trees and set about making it comfortable for the night. As we were preparing our campsite I saw GeeGee pushing several of the symbols on the back of her amulet. Not knowing what she was doing I set it aside and figured I would ask her about it later.

GeeGee then started telling us about the first expedition her Uncle Jonus had taken BeeBee and herself on a few years back. She also said she would explain the secret of Grouse Lake.

CHAPTER 10

The Secret of the Pink Crystal Revealed

"The secret of Grouse Lake?" Dora asked. "I didn't know Grouse Lake had a secret GeeGee. What kind of a secret is it?" She asked impatiently.

GeeGee looked at Dora and smiled. She understood a young girl's impatient attitude and decided she would have a little fun with her. She started her story.

"My people go to the surface world often. When we make these trips there are always three of us. We go in groups of three because our amulets have much more power when three of them are together. This gives us more safety against danger."

"When BeeBee and I became old enough, to make the trips to the surface world, Uncle Jonus took it upon himself to train us. He explained, in the deepest detail, how we were never to associate, in any way, with the surface people. He told us how the humans, if they saw us, would be afraid and try to kill or capture us."

"Uncle Jonus showed us how to use the power of our amulets to change our physical form into the creature you know as Bigfoot. While we are in our Bigfoot form our powers are limited."

"Our amulet still has the power to do many things, but it does not have as much power as it has in our world. He explained how we could tap the power, at our disposal, and showed us what it could do. With this knowledge we can easily avoid most confrontations with the humans."

"There are times, if we happen to loose our concentrations and if we are not paying attention to our surroundings, the humans can see us. This rarely happens, but it does happen."

"Is that what happened when your Uncle Jonus got shot?" asked Dora.

"Yes honey. Uncle Jonus was busy showing BeeBee and me how to survive and how to use the power of our amulets. We did not see the humans. The only thing that I can think of was the humans had been sitting in a tree, hunting, and we could not see or detect them. When they saw Uncle Jonus they shot and he went down wounded."

"What if Uncle Jonus had not been able to escape, what would have happened GeeGee?" asked Dora.

"If we are mortally wounded and die, our amulets have been preprogrammed to dematerialize taking their host with it leaving no remains what so ever."

"Wow." I remarked. "That must be why we have never found the remains of a Bigfoot."

"That's right Lester. If any of our remains were to be found the humans would not stop until they found our world and they would surely destroy us all. We have to be very careful because we will not harm a human under any circumstance."

"Now I shall continue my story. On our first trip to the surface world, Uncle Jonus took us to the cavern on Copper Mountain."

Again Dora interrupted. "I know why you come to our world GeeGee. Ladeena told us you have to gather crystals for your world."

"Yes Dora. Quartz and galena crystals are required in our world. Copper Mountain has an abundant supply and they are easy to gather. This is why our ancestors built the cavern and the tiny mounds to give us a point for returning to our world."

"You mean you can return to your world at any time?" I asked. "How come you have not returned to your world to get help in finding BeeBee?"

"Yes Lester, we can return home at any time only if we have our amulet. Without my amulet I could not return home to get help."

"The mounds were designed for inter dimensional travel only on the surface world. For us to return to our world we have to have, in our possession, our own amulet."

"If we get mortally wounded our amulet will take over and return us to a cave deep in the heart of a place you call Canada. There is a portal way back in the cave that opens up when A Hgiah comes close and this is where our amulet will place us. We are then drawn through the portal and the amulet sends a signal to our people and we are rescued."

"Dora," Lester excitedly remarked. "That must be the cave where you and I found Uncle Jonus's amulet."

"And do not forget the pretty old urn with the little pink crystal in it." Dora added.

"Urn, crystal, what are you talking about, Dora?" GeeGee sounded very excited.

Dora, seeing GeeGee's now escalated excitement, started getting very excited also.

"Yes," she said, "while we were in that old cave getting warm, I found this beautiful old bottle. Lester said it was an urn, whatever that means.

I put it in my dress to keep it safe. Lester told me to leave it because it might get heavy, but I kept it any way. There was something in it rattling around, but it would not come out."

"When I fell over the cliff, saving Lester, the bottle got broke and this round pink crystal fell out." Upon saying this Dora reached into her pocket and withdrew the round marble like crystal.

GeeGee let out a loud gasp. The sound of her gasping made cold deep chills run up and down my entire back. The chills were so intense I felt like I was freezing. Geegee was just standing there like she was in complete awe. Her mouth was open and her eyes were wide as saucers and unblinking. She was standing like a statue. What was happening?

GeeGee did not move. I felt her words rather then heard them. "Dora, you are holding the most sacred and precious relic in all Hgiah history."

"That small round pink crystal has more power contained in its small sphere then any thing else in our, or even your world. It disappeared many millenniums ago and has only been a hopeful legend to my people. If used by the right entity it has the power to accomplish absolutely anything. It even has the power to give complete peace and tranquility to all creatures and if used properly can allow us all to live as GOD intended like in the Garden of Eden."

"The pink crystal you hold in your hand is known as the (Creationism Stone). This stone contains the entire history of all creation."

Upon our receiving this wonderful revelation in the form of a telepathic communication, Dora very gently placed the crystal in GeeGee's hand. GeeGee smiled, took the crystal and placed it on her chest next to her heart where it immediately disappeared. GeeGee looked at us both with love in her eyes and said. "It is safe now, thank you."

CHAPTER 11

The Secret of Grouse Lake

With all the extreme excitement over the pink crystal I forgot about what GeeGee was telling us about Uncle Jonus and the secret of Grouse Lake. On the other hand, Dora was not about to forget that Grouse Lake held a secret and she blurted out. "Then what happened next, GeeGee?"

"What happened next?" GeeGee had a questionable look on her face.

"Yes, you were telling us about your first trip to the surface world with Uncle Jonus and you said Grouse Lake had a secret."

"Oh, yes, let's see now. Yes, it is important that you know the circumstances of how and why I am here."

"Uncle Jonus had taken us to the cavern on Copper Mountain, showing us the little mounds. He explained how they could be activated and what they could do. He said as we were to be explorers on the surface world, we needed to know all about what could possibly happen and how to protect ourselves at any given time."

"He showed us the opening on the rock wall and how it was the entrance to a cave that could take us to a small lake at the foot of Copper Mountain."

"That's Grouse Lake." Dora interrupted. "You said Grouse Lake had a secret?"

GeeGee looked at Dora for a second and then continued. "Yes Dora, Grouse Lake. This lake is important to us. It has a characteristic that no other lake, in this area, has. The lake is almost twice as large as it appears. The northwest half of the lake is covered with a thick layer of moss about two feet thick. This layer of moss hides this end of the lake."

"Is that the secret that you told us about earlier?" asked Dora.

"Well, that is part of the secret. The rest of the secret would not remain to be a secret if it were exposed now would it Dora?"

"Ohhhhhh." Dora whimpered. She sounded like she was disappointed, but I think she understood as she kind of smiled and did not ask any more questions.

GeeGee continued. "Now we have to get our thoughts together and start our search for my cousin. The last time I saw her, the hunter, that shot me in the leg, was carrying her into the forest. I followed them, but with my wounded leg I was unable to try to give her any assistance."

"Now that I have my amulet back and my leg is healed we need to find BeeBee as soon as possible. I am very concerned about her. That man, that took her, did not look very friendly."

CHAPTER 12

THE OLD MAN ON GROUSE MOUNTAIN

As we were preparing to leave our campsite, the crystal, that Jocko had given me, started vibrating. I reached down in my pocket and withdrew it. As I brought it forth it started shooting out rays of white light. As the light came forth a fan shape was formed and Jocko once again appeared.

We all stood perfectly still watching Jocko. He started turning slowly with his hand raised. As his arm came into a level position it stopped.

Jocko was pointing in a southerly direction and a red beam of light shot from his extended finger. The beam of light landed right at the summit of Grouse Mountain. Jocko disappeared.

I looked at GeeGee and was about to tell her about an old man that lived on top of Grouse Mountain, when Dora yelled.

"I know who lives up there," she screeched. "That's the old man Lester told me about. Lester said he's crazy and that he was never going up there again. He told me the old man tried to kill him. Isn't that right Lester?"

GeeGee looked at me with a smile and then asked me about the old man.

"It was last month. I was going up on Grouse to go hunting with Bozo. I had been hunting up there several times and had never seen him before. I had my 22 rifle with me, and my hunting knife. Bozo was running beside me."

"We had been hunting all the way to Grouse Lake and had not seen any game. The weather was beautiful so I decided to go up Grouse Mountain."

"It was early morning and I figured I had plenty of time to make it to the top of the mountain and back home before dark."

"It's a rough hike to the top, because the only trails are game trails. Bozo had been running in front of me and had scared several rabbits out of the brush. I raised my rifle, but they were moving too fast for me to get a good shot so I let them go."

"Just then Bozo started barking very loud. I figured he had a squirrel up a tree so I didn't pay any attention. Then he let out yelp and all was silent."

"As I started up the old game trail to look for Bozo, he jumped out of the brush and landed right on top of me. He started licking my face and I thought he had bitten me. The pain was excruciating. I felt my blood streaming down my face and slapped him off. He yelped and hit the ground hard. It was only then that I noticed something was wrong. There were porcupine quills sticking out of his nose."

"I grabbed him and apologized that I had hit him. He whined and again tried to lick my face. I stopped him before he was able to do so. I told him to lie down and he did. I then grabbed my knife and cut the ends of the quills off."

"After I cut the ends off, the quills were easy to pull out. Bozo yipped anyway, I think just because, and then started running around me in circles. He was sure happy."

"After loving on Bozo for awhile he finally settled down and I was able to clean the blood off my face. Boy it sure hurt."

"As I moved on up the trail, what there was of it, Bozo stayed right at my side. I think he figured that old porcupine was probably hiding somewhere up on the trail ready to ambush him again. I could see that Bozo was not at all ready for another go at the porcupine."

"The trail was really getting hard at this point. We had not even made it halfway up the mountain. There was very little game to be seen, but I decided since we had started up the mountain, I might as well go on to the summit."

"I had never been all the way to the top, but had heard it was beautiful and you could see all the way into Canada."

"As we continued up the mountain the trail disappeared. In front of us was a deep ravine. There was a creek at the bottom of the ravine about twenty feet down. There was no way to cross at this point so I made my way upstream."

"The ravine was getting deeper and deeper and I was about ready to give up and go back down the trail when I saw Bozo down at the creek. He was happily getting himself a drink. He must have felt me looking at him because he turned and barked at me. I think he was inviting me down. I made it down and up the other side and found the trail again."

"By this time we were almost to the top. As we rounded the next bend, we saw the strangest looking cabin."

"It was built on a cliff with some sort of shaft going down the rock wall in front.

"There was no glass in the windows and I decided no one lived there. There was a little stream below the cabin."

"I was thinking, since no one lived in the cabin, it would be fun to go in and explore."

"Just then something buzzed past my ear. Then I heard an explosion. Somebody had shot at me."

"Bozo started barking and I saw a huge giant of a man at the far end of the cabin. He had a long rifle in his hands and was raising it to his shoulder. As I saw him doing this, I ducked. Another bullet just missed me. I took off as fast as I could, calling Bozo as I ran. I came to the ravine and in my haste fell over the edge."

"I landed hard in the water, but luckily was not hurt to bad. Bozo was by my side barking. I somehow managed to make it up the other side of the ravine. Just as I got to the top, I saw the man again. He was again raising his rifle to shoot. I fell to the ground and he missed one more time. I heard him bellow out a few cuss words and he started running toward me."

"As I was able to get up, I took off like a shot not looking back. Bozo was way in front of me, barking at the top of his lungs. As I was running I was praying that the man would not be able to get over the ravine very fast and that I might be able to evade him."

"I ran until I was totally out of breath. I had been able to make it all the way down to Grouse Lake and knew where I could hide. I knew about a small cave up the hill a little ways and I could see the trail coming down from the mountain. I waited for a couple of hours, but he never appeared. When I felt it was safe I left the cave and went on home."

As I finished the story I felt GeeGee looking at me. She suddenly came toward me so fast that I did not have time to move. She grabbed me and swung me around several times laughing. I must have been at least ten feet off the ground and felt like I was breaking the sound barrier. "Lester," she excitedly said, "that must be the same man that took BeeBee."

"We have to go up there as soon as we can."

"That sounds good GeeGee, but it is getting late and Dora and I have to return home before dark."

"Oh my GeeGee, we were so excited about the moose I didn't even think about going home last night. Our parents are really going to be mad GeeGee. We have to go home right now."

GeeGee stood looking at me for a moment and then she softly laughed. "Lester, remember what we discussed earlier about dimensional travel? You are here at this moment, but to your parents you are there also."

"Wow. Yes I remember now, but it is so hard to comprehend GeeGee. How does it work?"

"Well, you do remember what the mounds in the cavern can do? The amulet can also do it on a smaller scale. The way it does this is it replicates a real dimension and induces an exact copy of the dimension in question in the mind of the person it is directed at. This gives the very real illusion of actuality and you, for all practical purpose, are in two places at the same time."

"My goodness, GeeGee, that's what you did when we escaped the moose and camped out below the lake. You made it look like we were home. I saw you pressing the symbols on the back of your amulet that night."

She looked at me and smiled and I knew I was right. GeeGee then said softly. "We better go."

"Well, lets get going then, were burning daylight don't you know." Dora quipped.

As we started up the old trail, going up Grouse Mountain, I thought to myself, leave it to Dora for the theatrics. She does not miss a cue.

CHAPTER 13

The Encounter, With Extreme Danger

As we were climbing the old game trail, I noticed several areas that looked different then when I was here before. The sides of the trail were beaten down more and it seemed wider. The birds were not singing and I found this very unusual. The birds were always singing. Something is wrong.

As I was deep in thought, I never noticed GeeGee and Dora were getting farther and farther ahead of me. When I finally realized that I was way behind, they were totally out of sight. I started walking a little faster. I thought I could catch them around the next corner. I was wrong. They were nowhere in sight.

I started walking faster not wanting to lose them. I just knew in my heart the old mountain man might be lurking on the trail up ahead.

I went around a couple more corners, but still no sign of Dora or GeeGee.

I had to warn them that we were getting pretty close to his cabin.

I called and called. I was really getting anxious by this time and started running up the trail.

I again called softly. No answer. Realizing I could not call out too loud, because the old mountain man might be close enough to hear me I had to keep my voice low.

After the confrontation I had had with him, I just knew he might be somewhere close and I did not want another confrontation.

Besides that, I remember when we were all at the grange hall last Easter Sunday. I had heard several of the local town folk talking about an old mountain man living in the woods.

The sheriffs department had followed him for miles, but had lost sight of him when he entered the woods. They figured he lived either on Grouse or Copper Mountain, but no one knew for sure. Folks that had seen him said he was a huge man and stood over eight tall.

He had been seen in town on several different occasions. Several weeks before the two girls were kidnapped; he had been seen lurking around the school.

They were saying that no one knew from where he came, but the authorities wanted him in connection with the kidnapping of two young girls. The assumption was that the man was an escaped convict known as Old Mad Jack.

WANTED

IN CONNECTION WITH THE KIDNAPPING
OF MARY AND SARAH

JACQUE PINSTIECHE
ALSO KNOWN AS
OLD MAD JACK
$10,000.00 REWARD
EIGHT FEET TALL, GREY BEARD & HAIR, MEAN AND VICIOUS, 300LBS +

The girls had been playing in back of the school in Troy and had just disappeared. Other children had seen a giant of a man lurking around the school several days before the kidnapping.

Everyone said that he did it. Everybody figured it was Old Mad Jack.

The local authorities had searched for weeks, but there were no clues. They had searched both Grouse and Copper Mountains many times, but had found no sign of him. The conjecture was that he had probably left the area. He was now listed on the nations most wanted list. A $10,000.00 reward was being offered for any information leading to his capture.

Once again loud crashing, in the brush behind me, interrupted my thoughts. My heart came into my throat as I heard a loud noise. I started running, not looking back. Whatever it was behind me, I did not want to know.

I knew I could not outrun whatever it was chasing me so I decided climbing a tree might be my only way to evade whatever it was. I saw a tall cedar tree with lots of branches that would afford me cover. I climbed up as far as I could go and stopped. I sat there perfectly still. I was up about twenty feet from the ground, so hopefully I would not be spotted.

I no sooner had settled down in my position than this huge bulking figure appeared on the trail below me. Sure enough it was Old Mad Jack and he looked even meaner then I had heard people say.

He was flailing the brush with a huge club. He had a knife on his side that looked like it was over a foot long. An old rifle was slung over his back. His hair was long and grey with black streaks and his clothes looked like they were made from animal skins. He looked like he was close to eight feet tall. He really looked mean.

As he passed under me, I was shaking so bad I just knew he could see the tree shaking below me. Sweat rolled off my face like a river. I thought about when Old One Ear had chased us when Dora and I were lost in Canada. I think I am as scared now as I was then. How can I warn GeeGee and Dora? I knew he was gaining on them fast. My adrenalin was really flowing, and my heart was beating so loud I just knew he would hear me.

All of a sudden my thoughts were interrupted when Old Mad Jack let out a mind boggling bellow. Harsh laughter was permeating the air like a blanket. Jack was now running up the old trail.

I stayed in the tree until I could no longer hear him. It must have been about ten minutes or more. I had to warn GeeGee and Dora, but had no idea how to do so. I knew if Old Mad Jack were to catch them it would be the end. This really scared me and I started moving faster.

Now GeeGee was in the lead. Dora was right behind her and they were moving fast. They had not noticed that I was not with them. GeeGee was heavily scrutinizing the trail in front of them watching for possible danger.

Dora, looking back, noticed that I was not behind them, suddenly grabbed GeeGee's hand. "GeeGee, I don't see Lester anywhere." This stopped GeeGee in her tracks. "Keep silent so that I may listen." She whispered. Dora stood perfectly still not even breathing.

"Do you think he is okay?" "Be quiet Dora, I need to see if I can hear anything." Dora put her head down, her feelings hurt. GeeGee had never been harsh with her before and Dora figured she was only trying to help, not realizing she was hindering GeeGee's concentration.

GeeGee, hearing something that sounded like laughter, told Dora to find a hiding place in the brush at the side of the trail. As Dora was entering the thick brush, something grabbed her feet and she was yanked high in the air. Yelling at the top of her lungs, Dora started crying. GeeGee, seeing what had happened, rushed over to help Dora. As she did so the earth underneath her feet gave way and she fell into a hole about thirty feet deep. GeeGee leaped up as high as she could, but could not reach the top edge of the hole. Dora was still dangling from the snare, crying, out loud.

Old Mad Jack, hearing the commotion up ahead, had slowed down and started moving quietly along the trail. He had heard Dora yell and knew that he had trapped her in his snare.

He had previously set the snare and dug the huge hole because he knew GeeGee would, eventually come try to rescue her cousin. He had been watching us for several hours before we had started up the trail. He did not know I was behind him.

I also had heard Dora yell. I had no idea what had taken place, but knew Dora was in trouble. I carefully made my way along the trail. I was being Very quite, knowing the old man was ahead of me. Then I heard a menacing laugh from up ahead. Old Mad Jack had found Dora.

I quietly snuck forward as fast as I possibly could without making any noise. As I rounded the next corner, I was able to see Dora hanging by her feet in the tree. I could not see Geegee anywhere and I was concerned for her. Old Mad Jack was busy pulling something out of the bushes. It looked like a big heavy duty net of some kind. I could see that it was made out of some kind of cable.

As I watched what he was doing, he threw the netting into a large hole. I heard a loud bellowing sound. It appeared to be coming out of the hole. Then I realized that GeeGee had been trapped also. What could I possibly do?

He then grabbed the rope that was holding Dora and pulled her down. Dora was kicking and screaming trying to get loose. This did not seem to bother him as he grabbed her and tied her up.

He then laid her aside and grabbed the netting and pulled GeeGee up out of the hole.

GeeGee had been thrashing around so much, trying to break free of the netting, that she was totally bound up and could not even move her arms.

After pulling the net up, with GeeGee in it, he grabbed another rope and looped it around Geegee several times making it virtually impossible for her to move. He then tied Dora to GeeGee.

He looked around several times as if he was searching for me. I stayed perfectly still afraid he might see me. After a few minutes he shrugged his shoulders and started pulling GeeGee and Dora up the old trail. He must have felt I was too small to be a threat.

I had no idea what I was going to do. He was right. I am just too small to be able to do much of anything to somebody as big as he is. I knew that I was going to have to outsmart him some way.

I followed Old Mad Jack as he proceeded up the trail. He was pulling GeeGee and Dora in the net behind him. I could hear Dora sobbing.

I could see the net bouncing off the rocks on the trail and just knew how much that had to be hurting the girls. He was not paying any attention to how rough the trail was and I knew he didn't care.

As we approached the ravine, he pulled out a long rope and threw it over a large branch of a pine tree on the other side. He tied the other end to the net. He then picked the net up, tightened up the rope, and tossed it, with GeeGee and Dora inside, across the ravine. The rope swung way past the tree and then started wrapping itself around the tree as it swung back. The rope wrapped itself around the tree trunk several times and as the net banged against the tree it stopped holding them tight. He then took a long run and jumped across the ravine.

He picked the net up, cut the rope that was still attached to the tree and started off toward his cabin.

I carefully made my way across the ravine and approached the cabin. I could hear harsh laughter coming from inside.

His roaring voice made me tremble. He was so huge I felt like a little mouse getting ready to attack a huge lion.

"LORD, please give me an idea on what I need to do and please give me the strength to do it."

I sat watching the cabin the rest of the day. Night was coming on and I was very tired. The noise inside the cabin had subsided by now and I wondered what was going on. I was hoping everything was okay and that Old Mad Jack had not hurt anybody.

I was fighting sleep. I knew I had to stay awake because I needed to be ready in case something would happen that might allow me too rescue GeeGee and Dora.

I noticed that I could cross the creek and crawl up the wooden shaft in front of the cabin without being seen. I did so and was able to get way up just under the window.

As I was pondering on what to do next, I saw movement out of the corner of my eye. It was still just light enough for me to see that it was a large grizzly bear.

The grizzly was approaching the cabin from the rear.

It appeared to be very curious as to what was inside the cabin. Just then I noticed Old Mad Jack coming out the front door. He had a water pail in his hand and had not noticed the grizzly. He slowly made his way down to the creek, as if he did not have a care in the world. He appeared to be singing, as he swung the pail back and forth and over his head like a child would do.

As Old Mad Jack reached down to fill his pail, the grizzly saw him. As the bear slowly ambled toward Mad Jack, I watched in awe. I was plenty scared as I was only about forty feet from Mad Jack, hanging on the old wooden logs below the window.

As I watched, Old Mad Jack stood up. He must have sensed danger or something wrong. He was looking straight at me. I did not move a muscle. It was getting quite a bit darker by now so I do not think he could see me, as I was in the shadows of the cabin. I do know one thing though. The grizzly bear was only about three feet from Old Mad Jack.

The grizzly had both front paws raised above his head and was about to come down on Mad Jack. When Old Mad Jack finally turned around the grizzly grabbed for him.

I figured seeing the Grizzly bear, towering over him with paws raised and three-inch claws extended, was not the most pleasant circumstances Old Mad Jack had ever experienced.

Just as the grizzly brought his huge paws down on him, Old Mad Jack ducked and wrapped his long arms around the bear. They fell over the edge into the creek. I looked up to Heaven and whispered a short prayer.

"Thank you, LORD, for sending help. Thank you."

I did not wait around to see if Mad Jack had escaped or not. The only thing that mattered to me was finding Dora and GeeGee. I climbed up the rest of the way and went through the window. They weren't there.

I didn't know what to do. I saw Mad Jack take them in the cabin and they had not come out. I searched everywhere, but there was no sign of them to be found.

The only door to the cabin was the one in front, so he could not have taken them out.

"LORD, please help me. I need to find them before Old Mad Jack returns if he escapes the grizzly and as strong as he is I expect him to do so. Please show me the way and guide me in the right direction."

After saying my prayer, I seemed to have a calmness come over me and I realized I had to slow down and think this out. There has to be an explanation. I checked all the walls, but found nothing out of the ordinary.

I was just about to exit the door to check around the outside of the cabin, when I heard a noise. It sounded like somebody had stepped on a twig and it broke.

I quickly looked around for a place to hide. There was an old barrel lying over in one corner and I headed for it. I had just got in when Old Mad Jack came through the door. Whew, that was too close. I thought to myself.

It was tight in the barrel and it stunk to high heaven. I don't know what had been in it, but it sure stunk.

I ventured a look out to see what he was doing. I saw that his shirt had been ripped to shreds. What was left was all bloody. He was tenderly washing his left arm with an old dirty rag.

As he finished washing he went over to one side of the room and lifted an old gunnysack off the floor. He picked up his rifle and a box of ammunition and then went outside. I could hear him moving around outside the cabin, busy doing something. After a short while I could no longer hear him, but decided to stay put for a while longer.

It must have been a least twenty minutes before I dared move, but it seemed like hours.

As I finally mustered up enough courage to crawl out of the barrel, Mad Jack suddenly came back through the door. I just barely made it back into the barrel before he had had a chance to see me.

He was carrying the huge Grizzly bear on his back as if it was a feather. He threw the grizzly down hard on the floor next to me. The bear's head fell right in front of the barrel opening. Mad Jack went back outside. I again started crawling out of the barrel, but was stopped short. The grizzly bear was not dead.

I ducked back into the barrel and watched as the Grizzly started to get up. He looked mad. Saliva was dripping down his jowls and his eyes were all bloodshot. He was breathing heavily and his breath was hot like a blast furnace as it engulfed my entire face. It stunk like nothing I had ever smelled before.

I noticed he had a large gash on the right side of his head. He must have only been knocked out and Mad Jack thought he was dead.

Just then Mad Jack came through the door. The grizzly saw him and let out the most horrifying growl I have ever heard. Before Old Mad Jack knew what was happening, the grizzly was on top of him. The bear had Mad Jacks head in his mouth and was biting down. I heard a terrible crunching sound and Mad Jacks body went limp. Mad Jack did not move.

The grizzly was not content that Mad Jack wasn't moving. He took Jacks body and threw it against the cabin wall. The cabin shook so hard I thought it was going to fall apart. Jack's body flew out the door and fell over the edge of the ravine into the creek and the grizzly followed. I could hear the grizzly bear making ferocious noises. He was still as mad as an angry hornet. I thought to myself, that bear must have really hated Old Mad Jack.

After closing the door I continued my search for GeeGee and Dora, hoping the grizzly would not return.

CHAPTER 14

I Find A Treasure Times Two

I had searched the whole cabin before Old Mad Jack had returned and I had found nothing. I knew I had to find where they could be because they probably had no food or water. I walked around the entire cabin inside and out.

There were no other doors anywhere. Wait a minute, I thought, what about the window I had came in through. I remember climbing up the side of the logs. It had seemed like some kind of shaft. It could be what I'm looking for.

I rushed into the little room where the window was, but there was no trap door in the floor as I had expected. I walked around the room several times, but found nothing. There had to be a way to get into that shaft.

I went outside one more time. Made my way down to the bottom of the shaft and searched all around the base. I could find nothing. I decided to crawl back up the side on the logs and enter the window as I had done previously. When I reached the top I started to go through the window. As I did so, I slipped and fell hard on the floor.

I hurt my knee as I fell, but forgot about it immediately as one of the boards on the floor broke. When I pulled the broken board loose I noticed that some of the floorboards were not nailed down. Wow, this is great. I started pulling the loose boards up and found a ladder going down the shaft.

I crawled down about half way when I saw a big opening cut out in the rock wall under the house. The opening was about ten feet high and eight feet wide.

There were lanterns, which were lit, along the sides of the walls about six feet up. The lanterns made the going very easy and I could see quite well. It looked like an old mine shaft from years gone by.

The shaft extended far back into the mountain forming a nice tunnel. This had to be where he had taken the girls. I took off on a run. There were lit lanterns every fifty feet or so. I must have gone into the tunnel at least two hundred feet or more.

The tunnel had been perfectly straight until now. It was taking a bend to the left and there were no lanterns. It was very dark, but I made my way carefully, and went on.

I had gone another hundred feet or so and could not see a thing. I decided that I should turn around and go back to get one of the lanterns when I heard a noise. It sounded like a little child crying. I listened intently, and then I heard it again.

I was very excited and cried out. "Hello, where are you?" There was dead silence. I hollered again. "Hello, can you hear me?"

Still there was no answer. I decided that I was just hearing things. Again, I started back for the lantern.

I took one off the wall and found it was completely full of kerosene. Old Mad Jack must have just filled them. With the lantern I went back into the tunnel where I had thought I had heard crying.

As I approached the area, I saw another tunnel taking off to the left. Thinking this might be where Jack had taken Dora and GeeGee, I proceeded down this tunnel. It was a bit smaller, but it was still big enough for a big man like Mad Jack.

I had gone about thirty feet when I again heard a noise. I stopped. I knew I had not imagined this and was determined to find out where it was coming from.

"Hello, hello, I am here to help you. Please answer." This time I got an answer. "Please help us, we need help."

"Puh-leeeease, help us." The voice was very faint and feeble. I did not understand. It was not Dora or GeeGee's voice. The voice sounded like it was coming from the wall at my left.

I pounded on the wall as hard as I could, but none of the rocks were loose. There was no way in. I stopped and thought about it for a minute and decided there had to be a room on the other side.

As I had walked through the tunnel to get here and I had not seen any openings anywhere. I figured there has to be a door further ahead.

I went on down the tunnel another twenty feet and found an opening. It was another tunnel. It was parallel to the one I had just left. As I walked in about twenty feet, the tunnel opened up into a small room.

As the light from the lantern illuminated the room, I gasped. There, in the corner, huddled together were two little girls about five or six years old. They were not moving.

"Jesus let them be okay. Lord please let them be okay."

They looked like they were starving. I reached down to help them stand up and found they were chained and locked to the floor. They were very weak, but they saw me and started crying out loud.

It was very dark and they could not see me too clearly. They must have thought I was Old Mad Jack, as they started begging me not to hurt them anymore. The older of the two girls, looked up at me with the most beautiful blue eyes I have ever seen and said, "we will do anything you say, just, please don't hurt us again."

Big tears were running down her pretty little face like rivers and her little lips were violently shaking. I just wanted to bawl, but knew I could not as it would surely hurt them more.

I turned the lantern so they could see my face and their crying turned into little whimpers of joy as they saw I was not Old Mad Jack.

They both tried to grab me, but could not because of the chains that were holding them to the floor.

"Help us mister, please help us." I broke out crying right there. I didn't know what to do. I knew I could not break the chain or lock. I had to leave them and go get help.

I tried to explain to them about the problem, but they just cried. "Please don't leave us mister. Please." This just broke my heart. I had to go and I knew it would be at least a day before I could make it back.

"Do you have any water mister?" I told them I did not, but I would get them some water and food. I had noticed that Mad Jack had some food in the cabin. I told the girls that I would be right back with some food and water. They both tried to grab me and asked me not to go. I had to get them the water and food so I left without looking back. They both burst out crying. Boy, that was hard leaving them, but I had no choice.

I ran all the way back to the shaft at the cabin, climbed the ladder and filled a sack with food. I found an old bottle, rinsed it out the best I could and filled it with water.

I flew down the ladder and ran all the way back where I left the girls. They were still crying until they saw me and they burst out laughing and crying at the same time. Boy, this was one of those moments.

The two kids just wolfed the food and water down. I cautioned them to slow down as not to get sick. They listened to me and started eating a little slower. They both had a hold on me, as if scared to death that I was going to leave them again.

I knew that I was going to have to leave them soon so that I could find GeeGee and Dora. GeeGee would be able to break the chain that held the two little girls. All this time, as I was thinking on what I needed to do, I knew there was a possibility I may not be able to find them at all. This concerned me greatly because I did not know how I would be able to get the two girls loose from the chains.

Thinking about this, I almost burst out crying again, but knew I better not. The girls were way too sensitive, at this moment, for me to start crying in front of them again.

"What is your name, mister?"

"My name is Lester."

"That is a beautiful name. Lester, I will always love you. My name is Mary and this is my friend Sarah." "We were so scared, and I thought we were going to die. That big man is so mean; I hope he doesn't come back. Did you see him, Lester? Did you see him?"

"Yes honey, I saw him. He will never hurt you again, I promise."

Sarah had been eating during this conversation I was having with Mary, but all of a sudden she looked up and said. "I love you too Lester. Thank you for saving us. Can we go home now? I miss my Mommy and she will be very worried."

Oh boy. That was the question I knew was coming and I was dreading it. I was not sure how I was going to answer without causing more hurt. I knew they were going to cry again, but I had no choice. I was going to have to go because I needed to find GeeGee and Dora, and get help for these two girls. I decided that now was the time. They had plenty of food and water and I would leave the lantern so they would have light. Maybe this might help so they would not be so scared.

"I cannot get you loose Sarah. I am going to have to go get help to break the chains."

"No Lester." They screamed together. "Please don't leave us."

I tried to explain the importance of getting help to break the chain. I told them I would leave the lantern for them to have light. I put the food and water right next to them.

After I explained, in great detail, why I had to leave, they both settled down a little bit.

They were exhausted after they ate and were feeling much better. I waited for a while, sitting next to them singing. After a short while, they both fell into a deep sleep.

I sat the lantern far enough away from them so they would not knock it over and quietly slipped out of the room.

I went back toward the front of the tunnel and got another lantern. I then continued deeper into the old mine tunnel.

My finding these kids, that Old Mad Jack had kid napped, and them still alive after more then two months, really made my hopes rise about finding GeeGee and Dora alive. I started running.

CHAPTER 15

I Find GeeGee and Dora

Running turned out to be both good and bad. As I was running, I rounded a corner and not seeing a rock on the floor, tripped and fell. The lantern hit the floor and shattered, making a loud noise that reverberated throughout the whole tunnel. That was the bad.

As the sound of the lantern shattering quieted down, another noise took its place. It was a humming sound like Dora and I had heard in the large cavern in Canada, after we had fell into the whirlpool.

As I was thinking about the sound and comparing, in my mind, the similarities of the two incidents, my crystal started vibrating. I pulled it out of my pocket and it lit up with a bright white light. It lit up the whole tunnel. I held it in the palm of my hand and it started rotating to the right.

When it stopped turning it was pointing straight down the tunnel that I had been following. I came to a place where there were two tunnels going in opposite directions. The crystal turned and pointed down the tunnel to the right.

The humming sound was now quite a bit louder, and I started getting excited. I went another fifty feet or so and the crystal turned again. This time, though, it was pointing at the rock wall. All of a sudden, the crystal turned red and got very hot. I dropped it on the floor.

As the crystal hit the floor big hot flames exploded upward, pushing me back about ten feet.

As I fell to the ground, wondering what had happened, the crystal engulfed the wall with some kind of beam. The wall just disappeared. The next thing I knew the crystal was back in my hand.

I was in absolute awe over what had just happened. I regained my senses fast and rushed over to the hole in the wall. The humming had stopped. My crystal lit up the room with a bright white light and I saw a large bundle over at the far side of the room. It was the netting that Mad Jack had thrown over GeeGee.

I reached down to see if I could move the bundle when something moved. It was Dora. She was still tied to GeeGee. She was barely moving. I was able to untie the ropes holding Dora and pulled her away from GeeGee. She let out a little moan and I knew she was still alive. I gave her some water and she took it graciously. She looked up at me and tried to smile. She was still too weak to say anything.

I gave Dora the bottle of water and went over to GeeGee. She had felt the movement when I had untied Dora from her and she now was trying to move.

She was really trussed up tight. Her hands were at her sides and she could not move them. She was totally unable to move in any direction. I had to try to remove all the netting myself. Luckily I still had my hunting knife. I started cutting all the ropes I could find. The netting was quite a bit looser now and GeeGee could move a little bit. I saw where one end of the netting had come loose so I concentrated on that. After about ten minutes I had cut through the rest of the netting and it peeled off easily. GeeGee was free.

As GeeGee rose she saw Dora on the floor. She immediately grabbed her amulet and went over to Dora. As she waved the amulet over her Dora started moving. Dora looked at me and softly said, "thank you Lester."

After GeeGee was through with Dora she turned toward me. Without saying a word she grabbed me and gave me the most loving hug I had ever had. She even kissed me as she said thank you.

As I turned from GeeGee, I heard Dora faintly ask, "How did you find us Lester?"

I told her that I would tell her later, but at this moment we had more important things to do.

"Come on, I will explain when we get there, but we have to move fast."

Geegee and Dora followed me as I ran down the old tunnel. As we approached the room where I had left Mary and Sarah, I asked them to be very quiet. They both looked at me with questionable looks on their faces, but they walked softly.

The two girls were still asleep. GeeGee, seeing the girls, rushed quickly over to them. She saw the chain immediately. She grabbed it and jerked it out of the floor. She then snapped it apart and the girls were free.

Both girls woke up at the same time, saw GeeGee, and started screaming. GeeGee backed off quickly and I took her place. The girls saw me and fell into my arms crying loudly.

"Lester, what is that beast? It's going to hurt us. Please don't let it hurt us Lester."

I was able to calm them down and explained that GeeGee was a good friend. They looked at me, not understanding how a beast that big could be a friend, but trusted me and let GeeGee look at them.

Geegee again brought forth her amulet and waved it over the two girls. They started looking better immediately. GeeGee then turned to me.

"Lester, that has to be the same man that took BeeBee. I know BeeBee has to be here in one of these old mine tunnels. We need to start searching right now. Dora, you stay with the girls and Lester and I will try to find BeeBee."

Mary and Sarah heard what GeeGee had said. They both looked at me. "Lester please don't leave us alone." I tried to explain to them that Dora would stay with them, but they would not hear of it.

I looked at GeeGee. She smiled and nodded her head. She and Dora took off down the tunnel.

I watched them go as they disappeared. I said a little prayer for their safety and asked God to help them find BeeBee, and that she would be okay.

CHAPTER 16

Mary and Sarah

I found a large rock with a flat top and sat down, not knowing how long the wait would be. I watched GeeGee and Dora disappear deeper into the old mine tunnel. Mary grabbed my arm, trying to get my attention. As I turned I noticed tears in her pretty, green eyes. "Lester, will that mean old man let us leave? His cabin is right on top of the mineshaft."

"Yes Mary, we will be able to go. The mean old man will never bother you again."

"Why did he take us, Lester? We were not doing anything to him. Me and Sarah were just playing on the teeter totter and he came and grabbed us.

He put this dirty old sack over my head and tied it closed. I could hardly breathe."

"Me to." Sarah blurted out. "I couldn't breathe either. He was really rough. He hurt my tummy and I couldn't see anything. It was scary. I didn't know what was happening. We were just playing and having fun. Momma's going to be mad at me Lester. She said I could only play with Mary for one hour and I know we have been gone longer then one hour. Will you tell my momma that I couldn't come home because that mean old man had me Lester? I do not like spankings and when I don't do as I am told my momma will spank me. Please, Lester, please tell my momma why I could not come home."

Sarah started crying again. I reached over to give her a hug and she fell into my arms and just cried and cried. Mary was watching with big tears streaming down her face. I extended my hand toward her. She grabbed it, pulling herself toward me, and threw her arms around me again and burst out crying also. "We love you Lester."

I sat there with both girls in my arms. They just cried and cried. This was an extremely heart breaking moment for me.

I started singing a song, and the girls were crying less. I rocked back and forth and continued humming, thinking about these two pretty little girls and the ordeal they had been through. This would have been rough on anybody, but two little girls like this. I knew this terrible thing would be in their minds forever, and it just broke my heart.

Sarah had long blonde hair and beautiful deep green eyes. Her little face was full of freckles over the bridge of her nose, which was dainty. She had on a pair of light blue knickerbockers with a white stripe down the sides of both legs. Her shirt was also light blue, except the sleeves which were white with a light blue stripe down the sides of each one. Her shoes were white penny loafers.

Mary was also a blonde. Her hair was long, hanging down past her shoulders. Eyes so blue I felt that I could fall right into them. She also had freckles, over a tiny upswept nose. She had on a yellow sweater. Her pants were yellow with a big bow in the back. She also had on white penny loafers. They looked like could be sisters.

CHAPTER 17

BeeBee is Found

As I was rocking the girls back and forth, they both fell into a deep sleep. Lord only knows they needed it with what they had gone through. It would have been a traumatizing time for anybody not alone two little girls.

Deep in thought about things that had happened the last couple of days, I had not noticed the crystal in my pocket was vibrating. I think the crystal had a mind of its own, as it started getting hot. Wow, I knew it wanted something now. It had my full attention as I pulled it out of my pocket.

The crystal cooled off immediately and started glowing. I sat it on the rock next to me and it sent a white fan like light toward the ceiling. As I watched, a picture started forming. Wow, I could see GeeGee and Dora as they were making their way through the old mine tunnel. I felt like I was walking with them.

I noticed, as the crystal was showing me, that the tunnel had again gotten smaller. There were quite a few small rocks scattered all over the floor. Along one side were several big boxes that had danger, explosives written on the sides. I surmised they must have contained dynamite.

I noticed a corner going to the right. Just ahead was a large cavern. The cavern appeared to be about forty feet wide and about eighty feet long. Right in the center of the cavern was a large rock platform. The platform was flat on top. It was about three feet wide and ten feet long. The top of the platform was about three feet off the floor. Hovering over the platform was a large spherical shaped object.

The round object looked to be about three feet in diameter, and had six large green crystal type objects circling it like moons. Each one was glowing with a bright bioluminescent glow.

At the far end of the cavern was a large hole in the floor. The hole was very deep and about fifteen feet in diameter. A tremendous amount of heat was coming out of the opening. At the very bottom of the hole was a pool of bubbling lava. I think this must be some kind of ancient sacrificial chamber. It gave me the eeriest feeling.

The scene then changed, as I was watching the holograph, and the wall of the cavern appeared. A huge boulder, about ten feet high was sitting on the floor. The boulder was approximately two inches from the wall. Looking closer I noticed there was some kind of opening behind the boulder. I watched as GeeGee tried to move the boulder. It would not budge.

I saw Dora slowly move toward the boulder. She was pointing at a depression in the rock wall.

She put her hand on the depression and pushed gently. The huge boulder slowly started moving aside. "Wow. Way to go Dora." I yelled.

I felt movement in my lap and realized that I still had two precious bundles sitting there. I had almost woke them up. I needed to be more careful. The girls needed their sleep.

As my attention returned to the scene developing in front of me, I saw that the boulder had been hiding a narrow hole in the wall. As GeeGee squeezed through, Dora followed. The passage was about ten feet long and then opened up into a small pitch-black room. Dora had the lantern, and as she came through the narrow passage into the room, her lantern illuminated a horrible scene. At the far end of the room was a figure hanging on the wall.

The figure had both arms tied way above its head. The legs were tied spread-eagled. GeeGee finally was close enough for me to see clearly. It was BeeBee.

GeeGee released the shackles that were holding BeeBee to the wall. She then carried her through the narrow shaft into the large cavern. She went over to the rock platform in the center of the room and gently laid her down.

Both of BeeBee's arms had been tied together in the back of her neck so she could not move them in any manner. This had to be extremely painful.

BeeBee had lost so much weight; she looked like skin and bones.

GeeGee took her amulet, pushed a few of the symbols, and swept it over BeeBee. There was no response. GeeGee repeated the process and there still was no response.

"Please LORD, let BeeBee be okay," GeeGee prayed.

There still was no response. BeeBee did not move.

By this time, GeeGee was crying. She sat down on the platform and hugged BeeBee. She just sat there rocking back and forth crying. GeeGee's crying was the most sorrow-full thing I have ever heard. All the time, as she was rocking with BeeBee in her arms, I could see she was praying.

I watched in absolute horror as the scene unfolded before me. I felt so helpless.

Dora, watching GeeGee, gently grabbed BeeBee's arm and felt for any pulse. There was none. BeeBee was dead.

GeeGee, being able to regain a small amount of composure, gentle picked BeeBee's limp lifeless body up and started walking toward the opening leading back to where I was waiting.

I woke the girls up so that we would be ready to go when GeeGee and Dora had caught up with us. We went out into the main tunnel and waited.

It was only a few minutes later when GeeGee appeared. I let her pass to lead the way out. When we finally reached the cabin, it was starting to get dark. I had grabbed two more of the lanterns as we passed them so we had plenty of light.

GeeGee laid BeeBees' lifeless body on the floor of the old cabin, and sat there just staring at her, crying. I told Dora and the girls we should quietly go lie down and try to get some sleep and not bother GeeGee.

It was very hard for me to sleep that night, but finally did so. I had said a long prayer to GOD before falling asleep, and I knew that he would prevail.

I fell into a deep sleep and started dreaming. I woke with a start the next morning and the sun was already shining. I had been dreaming about the Creationism Stone. Wow, "GeeGee, GeeGee, GOD has given me the answer."

GeeGee was still sitting by BeeBee in the middle of the floor and had not heard me. I rushed over to her and touched her on the shoulder. GeeGee looked up at me with tremendous pain all over her face. Before I could say another word, she grabbed me and started crying again. I gave her a great big hug and kissed her cheek. "GeeGee," I said softly. "GOD has given me the answer in a dream."

"The answer, in a dream?" GeeGee looked at me with a question on her face. "What do you mean Lester?" she asked.

"The Creationism Stone, GeeGee."

GeeGee jumped up so fast, I was tumbled clear across the room. "Yes Lester, the Creationism Stone, wow, Dora, I need the Stone, Dora where do you have it?"

GeeGee was showing so much excitement, it spread to the rest of us like lightning. We were all having trouble thinking, but Dora was finally able to tell GeeGee that she had the Stone. GeeGee, remembering what she had done with the Stone, pulled it from its safe place and went over beside BeeBee.

GeeGee immediately took the stone and laid it on top of BeeBee. As it laid there nothing happened. We all stood watching, but there was no activity or anything taking place. I did not understand. My dream indicated that the Creationism Stone could perform miracles. I thought sure it would bring BeeBee back to life. What's wrong?

Geegee started crying again.

Dora was in the corner praying.

Mary and Sarah were beside her and praying also.

I went over to GeeGee to comfort her. I put my arms around her and started praying.

"Oh Precious Heavenly Father. I come to you God with my entire heart and soul. I know Lord; you are all powerful and can do all things. All you ask of us is to believe and follow your commandments. Please Lord, pour your most gracious love on us and heal BeeBee. I know Lord all things are possible for you for those who believe and trust in you. We love you God. We humbly ask these things in your precious Sons name. Amen."

As I finished my prayer, the little pink crystal started glowing. The crystal intensified its glow and was so bright we could not look at it. The whole room was brightly lit up.

All of a sudden it felt like the whole room exploded as a tremendous ray of light, not unlike lightning, shot from the sky, engulfing BeeBee in its powerful light. Then all of a sudden everything seemed to be the way it was previously.

BeeBee was still lying on the table motionless. What had just happened? GeeGee again started crying and bowed her head in her arms.

The next moment the most wonderful thing took place. BeeBee sat straight up. "Does anybody have any water? I am so thirsty."

We all jumped in absolute wonder. BeeBee was alive. We all started crying and laughing at the same time.

We were all thanking GOD for his precious mercy.

"Thank you Lord. Thank you."

BeeBee looked around. "GeeGee, where are we? Who are all these kids? Why are you all laughing and crying at the same time? What's going on? Oh, I feel so hungry. I feel like I just woke up. I had a terrible dream GeeGee. I think it was a dream. Why am I so skinny? Oh, GeeGee, I'm so tired."

Upon saying this, BeeBee started teetering like she was about to pass out. We all rushed over and grabbed her to keep her from falling.

GeeGee sat down on the floor and laid BeeBee's head in her lap. "You rest right now BeeBee. I will explain when you wake up. Here, drink this water first and then go to sleep.

BeeBee immediately went to sleep.

CHAPTER 18

BeeBee Tells Her Story

BeeBee slept peacefully for several hours. Dora looked around the cabin for some food of some sort. There were several cupboards at one end of the room and one of them was full of dried fruits and nuts. The other cupboard was full of jerky. There was a can that had some funny smelling things in it. Dora showed GeeGee the can and she said it was dried mushrooms.

There was plenty to eat.

It was early afternoon before BeeBee woke up. When she did so she was a little more coherent, but still did not remember what had taken place the last few days.

GeeGee started explaining who Dora and I were and that we had been in their world and had met their parents and grand parents.

She told her how Old Mad Jack had captured them and the terrible things that he did. As GeeGee was explaining about Old Mad Jack, BeeBee interrupted. "Yes, I remember now. Boy he was sure mean to me and the way he had me tied up, I couldn't even move. How did you rescue me?"

GeeGee explained how I had been able to find them and how Old Mad Jack had met his end.

BeeBee interrupted at this point. "You know GeeGee, I do not like to see any bad thing befall any one, but I feel this Mad Jack got what was coming to him."

BeeBee said she was hungry, so Dora went to the cupboard and brought out the fruits and jerky. GeeGee saw the jerky and asked what it was. Dora told her that it was jerky and it tasted good. GeeGee looked at it a little closer, than asked what it was made from. Dora said she thought it was made from dear meat. GeeGee handed it back to Dora and told us they did not eat meat. "We do not kill any living thing, Dora, so we do not eat meat."

That was okay with Dora and me. We sat and munched down on the fruits and mushrooms and had a good meal.

As we were eating, BeeBee started telling us what had happened to her when Old Mad Jack had captured her.

"I remember when I saw the big elk go down, I just lost it. I was so angry I wasn't thinking. All I knew is that the big man had killed that poor animal, and I could see no reason for it. I could feel the elks pain, as it laid there dying."

"The last thing, I remember, was that the man had raised his gun and hit me hard in the head.

When I woke up, I found my arms tied, above my head. He had raised my arms up in such a way that I could not even turn my head.

My hands were in back of my neck and ropes were tied around both wrists. He had pulled the ropes forward and around my neck under my chin. I tried to get my arms free but could not. I could not even reach my amulet for aid. Any movement I made choked me."

Dora interrupted at this point. "How come your amulet did not send you back to the cave in Canada, BeeBee?"

"The only time our amulet takes over and sends us to the cave, is when we are mortally wounded Dora. I was not wounded, just unconscious."

BeeBee then continued.

"He then tied a rope from my wrists down to each one of my ankles. Another rope was tied to my wrists also. It was about 12 feet long. This rope he used to control me. A slight tug and I could not breathe. I was totally at his mercy."

"Leaving the cabin was out of the question. The terrain beside the cabin was so rough, that if I had tried I would have fallen to my death. The big man knew this and was not afraid to leave me alone for days. He did so on many occasions."

"Several months ago he left for three days. He returned around midnight on the fourth day. I was asleep when he came into the cabin. He was being very quite for some reason. I woke up just as he dropped two gunnysacks in the old shaft over there. The sacks had something in them because I saw movement. Then I heard sounds like children crying."

Dora, all of a sudden, interrupted. "That was Mary and Sarah!" she exclaimed. "They told us that Old Mad Jack had put them in gunnysacks."

Mary and Sarah both whimpered when Dora said this. Dora sat up straight and realized what she had said. "I am so sorry. I never thought, when I brought that up. I some times blurt out my thoughts before I realize what I am saying." Upon saying this, Dora got up and hugged the two girls. She sat down and they both crawled on her lap.

BeeBee continued. "He disappeared down the shaft and did not come out until next morning."

"Old Mad Jack, you say? That sure fits him. I never did know his name. He never spoke to me even once. I could not figure out why he kept me here all this time."

"A little over a month ago the man, oh that's right, you said Old Mad Jack. Old Mad Jack rushed out side the cabin with his gun. I heard three shots. He then came back into the cabin cursing loudly. I did not know what was happening. He grabbed me roughly, and threw me down the shaft. I landed hard and it really hurt. He then came down after me and drug me far back into the old mine tunnel."

"We passed through a large cavern that had a big table in the center of the floor. There was a hole, at one end of the cavern. The hole had a bright orange light coming from it. The cavern was very hot inside. There was a large boulder at the side of the wall. He easily moved it aside. He dragged me through this narrow opening into a small room and tied me on the wall. That is the last I can remember, until I saw you."

"My goodness," Dora blurted out. "No wonder you're so skinny. You must not have had anything to eat or drink all that time. How cruel!"

BeeBee just nodded her head and didn't say any more.

CHAPTER 19

We Meet Old Mad Jacks Bear

By now the day was about over. GeeGee said that we had better get some rest. We would be having a big day tomorrow. She told the girls and us to lie down and go to sleep. She and BeeBee than went outside. We did not see them again until morning when they woke us up.

GeeGee said that we needed to go now. We all got up and went outside. Looking east, over the mountain, we saw a beautiful sunrise. The sky was perfectly clear. It was going to be a beautiful day.

BeeBee was waiting for us outside by the creek. She took GeeGee aside for a moment and whispered something in her ear. She was speaking too low and I could not hear what she said, but GeeGee looked back at us and nodded her head. She then motioned for us to follow.

When we got to the edge of the ravine, GeeGee picked Dora and me up and jumped over the ravine. BeeBee did the same with Mary and Sarah. They then set us down and we started down the old trail.

I couldn't help but notice that GeeGee, every once in a while, glanced back on the trail that we had just left. I did not know why, but figured BeeBee had seen something back at the cabin.

We made it all the way down the mountain without further incident. GeeGee was still watching behind us.

All of a sudden, she and BeeBee grabbed all of us and took us into the brush. They made us lay down and told us not to move or make a sound of any kind. GeeGee said our lives depended on it. They then came very close to us and gently started blowing their breath on us. They both then laid down beside us.

We could see the trail where we had been previously. We must have laid there silently for fifteen or twenty minutes, it seemed like hours, and then we heard some deep grunting.

A big grizzly had been following us down the trail. I then knew what BeeBee had whispered to GeeGee up at the cabin. No wonder they were in such a hurry to get us down that trail.

The grizzly bear was sniffing the air. It appeared that he had lost our scent. He was going around in circles, looking everywhere.

The grizzly stayed in the area searching. He must have known his prey, (us), must still be here somewhere. As we laid there, in total silence, the bear came straight toward me. His head was about a foot from mine. I could hardly handle the stench. It was all I could do to contain my fright. He sniffed a few times, but appeared not to be able to smell me. Boy, his head was bigger then my whole body.

He had to be as big as Old One Ear.

He circled a few more times. Stood up on his hind legs and let out a loud bellow.

I guess he figured he had shown us who the boss was. He then ambled off into the forest.

To me he looked like the same bear that had taken Old Mad Jack.

We stayed there for about an hour before moving. Geegee then rose up and motioned us to be silent and follow her.

I could see Dora was about to ask a question. I motioned to her to be silent. She gave me a funny look, stuck her tongue out at me then shrugged her shoulders and didn't say a word. She knew I was right and her question could wait until later. Right now getting as far from the grizzly as possible was the most important thing we could to do.

CHAPTER 20

We Meet The Sheriff of Lincoln County

GeeGee was in the lead. Mary and Sarah were right behind her. Dora was next with me following. BeeBee had taken up the rear, just in case the Grizzly decided he wanted to have some more fun with us.

By this time we had made it down to Grouse Lake, and were just about to cross a wide meadow above the lake. GeeGee, all of a sudden, stopped and motioned for us all to be very quiet.

She was looking across the lake as if she had noticed something on the other side.

She pointed and all of our eyes followed in that direction. Sure enough, there were three figures coming our way. It was the Lincoln County sheriff and three deputies.

GeeGee knew that Mary and Sarah had to be taken home and this looked like a good opportunity for them to get home safely.

She also knew that explanations would have to be made. She told Dora and me to wait and go with the sheriff.

"What about you and BeeBee getting back to your home?" I asked.

"I will be in contact with you after the two girls are home safely. You and Dora will need to stay home for one day, and then come back up to the old mine. I will know when you arrive and BeeBee and I will be there waiting for you."

"You Lester, have the only means for us to return home. The crystal that our grandfather Jocko placed in your trust, will allow us to do just that. He will explain what has to be done and how to do it when the time comes. Guard it well, Lester."

"Oh, and all will be as it should be when you get back to your homes."

Upon saying this GeeGee and BeeBee hurriedly took off for the cave.

As the sheriff and his deputies got closer, Dora and I started yelling to attract their attention.

They saw us right away and started running toward us.

As they approached they started getting excited. One of the deputies was a woman. She immediately picked up Mary and Sarah, and they both started crying.

The sheriff looked at us and started asking questions. "Where did you find these two girls? We have been searching for them since before Easter."

I told him how we had been on Grouse Mountain exploring and about Old Mad Jack and how we had found the two girls tied up in the old mine.

I explained how the huge grizzly had chased us and how big he was. As I mentioned the grizzly bear, Dora spoke up excitedly. "And the bear ate Old Mad Jack!" She exclaimed.

"And the bear did what?" asked the sheriff.

"He ate Old Mad Jack." Dora repeated. "He grabbed Mad Jacks head in his great big mouth and crunched down. Lester said he heard a horrible crunching sound and Old Mad Jack and the bear fell over the edge of the ravine."

"That was the last we saw of Old Mad Jack. I know the bear ate him, cause he looked hungry. You can ask Lester, he saw it happen."

The sheriff looked at me for a moment. He then asked. "Can you take us to that spot young man?" I told him that I could.

The sheriff then turned to the lady deputy. "Joan, will you take the girls back to town and notify their parents. John and I will go on up the mountain to verify what these kids have told us. Oh, take this young lady also. I think the boy can lead us okay."

Dora, hearing that she had to go back to town, let out a little whine, but followed the lady deputy anyway.

Deputy Joan was very pretty. She stood about five feet two with beautiful deep brown eyes and long brunette colored hair.

She had kind of a slight build. I thought to myself, she looks like she's about as feisty as Dora.

Deputy Joan had on a pair brown slacks and a brown shirt. A blue scarf was around her neck and she was carrying a double barrel shotgun.

The sheriff looked at me. "What's your name young man?" I told him my name and he sort of smiled. "You can call me Mike." He said. "And this is John, and this young man is Dave," as he pointed at the two deputies.

The sheriff was a big man about six feet tall and looked like he weighed at least three hundred pounds.

He had a large mustache that was trimmed neatly and each side came to a well-groomed point. He also had a neatly trimmed gray beard about three inches long.

His hair was gray and hung down just above his shoulders.

His eyes had a very kind look to them. I liked the sheriff right off the bat.

Deputy John was a tall man. He looked to be about six and a half feet. He had short cut blonde hair, neatly combed straight back and receding a little in the front. He seemed to be always smiling.

He was wearing an old brown jacket that had seen better days. It appeared to have been made out of an old deer skin. He had on a pair of jeans that looked new. He carried a big pistol on his hip.

Deputy Dave looked to be about five and a half feet tall. He was stout and must have weighed about 240 pounds. He was bald and had a kindly face.

He was wearing a pair of old jeans and had a pistol strapped to his waist. I thought to myself, as he came over to say hi, I bet he could handle himself in any type of situation.

I was roused out of my thoughts, all of a sudden, by the sheriff's deep voice. He had seen me looking at the pretty young deputy. He just winked at me, as if he thought he knew what I was thinking, and said, "Let's get up that mountain, young man. I want to see what took place up there."

I looked back to wave to Dora, but they had already disappeared from sight so I took off behind the sheriff. The two deputies were right behind me.

The sheriff, for being such a big man, could move through the brush pretty fast. I had a hard time keeping up with him. He looked back several times and asked if I was doing okay. I told him yes, I was fine, not wanting to slow him down.

When we finally caught up with the sheriff, he was standing beside the big hole that Old Mad Jack had trapped GeeGee in. Sheriff Mike was standing there scratching his head, as if he was trying to figure out the significance of the hole.

As the deputies and I got closer, Deputy Dave exclaimed, "looks like somebody wanted to trap something really big sheriff. That hole is so deep it could hold a huge grizzly."

I wanted to tell them how GeeGee had been trapped in the hole, but knew I could not.

When Deputy Dave mentioned grizzly, I thought I heard a grunt behind us. I listened intently, but did not hear it again, so I set it aside without mentioning it. I later realized that was a mistake. I should have said something.

After looking the hole over, the sheriff decided to go on. As before, he was moving fast. He got several hundred feet ahead of us. I could hear him grumbling up ahead, and figured he had come to the ravine and was trying to figure out how to get down and to the other side. We caught up with him in short order. He was just standing there scratching his head again.

I asked him to let me lead, because I knew the easiest way to get down. He consented, and I said, "Follow me". We made it to the other side without any mishap.

As we crested the other side of the ravine, I heard the grunting sounds again. I looked to see if the sheriff or the deputies had heard it, but they had not. I mentioned it to Deputy John, but he said he had not heard anything and it was probably just my imagination. I knew better, but again decided not to pursue it.

The sheriff, by this time, was able to see the old cabin. "Wow, come look at this John. You're not going to believe what this guy built up here. This is some cabin, and look how it's protected from all sides against any intruders. This guy must have lived here a long time."

The sheriff then turned to me. "Where did you last see this Mad Jack fellow?" he asked.

I showed them where the bear had grabbed Old Mad Jack, and how they had gone over the hill down to the creek.

The sheriff took off over the hill down to the creek. Looking back over his shoulder, he told the deputies to look inside the cabin for any clues to the identity of Mad Jack.

I took the lead into the cabin and both deputies followed me. I showed them the little room that had the shaft going down to the old mine. Just then we heard the sheriff holler. "John, Dave, come out here and look at this."

"What do you make of it?" The sheriff asked, as he showed them Old Mad Jacks leg with the boot still on it. "I found this and one thumb. Maybe, if the guy was ever finger printed, we can determine who he was. It looks like we won't have any more children being kidnapped by him."

The sheriff turned toward me and said. "You realize, young man, there is a ten thousand dollar reward for the return of those two girls and another ten thousand for the apprehension of the kidnapper. Looks like you kids might be the ones to collect."

We started back down the hill.

CHAPTER 21

We Meet The Grizzly Bear Again

Deputy John had found an old canvas bag and he put Old Mad Jacks leg and thumb in it for safe keeping. He tied the canvas bag around his waist and said, "This will keep it safe until we get back to the office."

The sheriff always seemed to be in such a hurry. As we climbed out of the ravine he was already out of sight. Deputy Dave told me that the sheriff probably wanted to check out the hole for any more clues to what Old Mad Jack had trapped there.

As we trod on down the trail we could hear the sheriff. Holler. "John, you better come look at this. I have never seen anything like this in my born days. Look at this hair. It has to be at least twelve inches long, and look at the color. It's red. And you need to smell it. It has a real musky smell to it. This did not come from any old bear."

Sheriff Mike was holding up a handful of GeeGees hair. Oh my goodness, I thought, what am I going to do? I can't let them find out about GeeGee and BeeBee. This could really be a problem

The sheriff handed the hair to Deputy Dave. The deputy took it and held it up to his nose. "Your definitely right Mike, this is not bear hair. I saw hair like this one time when I was fishing up on Fisher River just east of Libby."

"I had hiked way up the river several miles. I do this because the fish are huge up there where no one goes fishing. I had just started fishing back down stream when I heard this mind boggling roar. It sounded like a cross between an African lion and a Kodiak bear. It just curdled my blood."

"Right after I heard this roar, I came upon this makeshift shelter of some sort, made from several downed trees. The floor of the shelter had a deep layer off moss on it."

"There was a large pile of mushrooms on one side of the shelter and a pile of pinecone seeds on a layer of cedar branches. A few strips of white spaghetti looking things were lying next to the mushrooms. These I knew, from my boy-scout days, were the inner strips of a pine tree. Whatever or whoever was staying here was sure eating well."

"As I looked in the makeshift doorway I found hair, just like this. I figured it was from a Sasquatch."

"I think Old Mad Jack caught a Sasquatch here in his trap."

The sheriff looked at Deputy Dave as if he thought the deputy had lost it.

"A Sasquatch? Up here? You have to be kidding. I have never heard of a Bigfoot in this area."

Deputy Dave looked at me, smiled, and stuck the hair in his pocket.

We had only gone another hundred yards or so down the trail when we heard the sheriff holler again. This time though it was a very distressed, almost scared holler."

"Be careful back there. I just saw that big grizzly the kid told us about. It may be the same one that ate Jack. He's just to the side of me."

As we heard Sheriff Mike yell this out we also heard the grizzly let out a loud growl.

Several shots rang out and then there was a deep silence. All the birds had quit chirping and there were no sounds at all except the slight breeze rushing through the trees. We hurriedly made our way down the path, but there was no sign of the sheriff anywhere.

Then, in the middle of the trail, I spotted the sheriffs pistol. There was blood all over the handle and I just knew the Grizzly had got the sheriff. I was really concerned because I knew how mean the bear was. The sheriff was probably dead.

Deputy Dave grabbed me roughly, picked me up and without saying a word started running down the trail. I knew he figured the same as I, that the sheriff was gone and we had to get out of there. Deputy John was right behind us.

Deputy Dave must have run about a mile, because when he stopped we were at the edge Grouse Lake.

"We have to get back to town and send out a search party for the sheriff," he said. "There's nothing we can do by ourselves, at this time, so let's get going."

"John, you stay here just in case the sheriff comes down."

Boy, we made it in short order. I have never come down from Grouse Lake as fast as we did that day. We stopped briefly at my house so that I could explain to my mom what had happened. Deputy Dave told her that I needed to go with him and that we had to hurry so that maybe he could get the other deputies together and get back up Grouse Mountain and hopefully save the sheriff. Upon saying this, he grabbed me, threw me in his car and took off.

My mom, stunned by what had just happened, woke my stepfather up and they followed the deputy and myself to town.

When we arrived in Troy, there were several deputies waiting for us at Kennslers market. Dave had called them on his radio to save time. One of the deputies grabbed me and told me they had to take me to Libby to talk to the authorities about Mad Jack and Mary and Sarah's kidnapping.

Deputy Dave and the other deputies then took off for Grouse Mountain.

My mother and stepfather pulled up just as they were putting me in the car.

"Where are you going with my son?" she asked somewhat angrily. Not knowing what had taken place, my mom did not understand why they were taking me to the sheriffs' office. This was starting to make her more irate. One of the deputies, I think her name was Sally, explained to my mom what they needed to question me about. She told my mom they could follow the sheriffs' car and then, when I had answered all the questions, they could take me home. This satisfied my mom and we proceeded to Libby.

CHAPTER 22

Sheriff Mike Almost Dies

It was after ten p.m. when we finally got home. I had wanted to talk to Dora, but mom told me it would have to wait until morning.

Next morning I was up early. I got all my chores done and was ready to go over to Dora's house when momma called me to come in for breakfast. I told momma I was not hungry, but she told me I had to eat anyway. I started to wolf it down as fast as I could. Momma told me to slow down. "Nothing is so important that you have to make yourself sick over it," she said.

I finally finished my breakfast and asked if I could be excused and if I could go over to Dora's house. She said I could and I started out the door, almost running right over Dora.

"Wow, you're here early!" I exclaimed. "Yes, and we're burning daylight don't you know," Dora quipped.

"Yes I know Dora and I realize we have to get back to GeeGee and BeeBee as soon as possible."

"GeeGee and BeeBee?" Who are GeeGee and BeeBee? Has somebody new moved into our Iron Creek area?" Momma asked.

Oh boy. Momma had heard us talking about GeeGee and BeeBee. What could I say? I have never lied to my mom and I'm not going to start now, but I couldn't tell her about GeeGee and BeeBee, not yet. What am I going to say?

Dora immediately came to my rescue when she burst out, "Lester, you don't have to pretend you have two girl friends just to try and make me jealous. Now if we are going to go have fun exploring, don't you think we had better get moving?"

This must have satisfied my mom, because she just smiled and closed the door without waiting for an answer from me. "Thank you Dora," I mumbled to myself. I do not know if she heard me or not, but she said, "Your welcome Lester." And off she went, running as fast as her little legs could carry her up the trail.

It was another beautiful day, not a cloud in the sky. We were able to get up to the old mine without any problems.

As we approached the old mine my crystal started vibrating again. I pulled it from my pocket and it just continued to vibrate. I did not understand until I saw GeeGee and BeeBee approaching.

We heard dogs barking further up the hill. "The posse must be coming back Lester. Maybe we better hide."

Before we had a chance to call out to GeeGee, I looked over where I had seen them and they were gone. I told Dora there was no reason for us to hide because nobody was after us, and besides that GeeGee and BeeBee were hid where they could not be found.

The posse had got close enough to us now that we were able to see they had the sheriff on a stretcher. He was not moving and I was concerned about him. Dora and I watched as they drew closer to us. Deputy John was in the lead and he was limping very badly.

The dogs saw us and rushed over happily for us to pet them. I think they thought they knew us.

About then Deputy John saw us. "Hey kids, what are you doing up here?"

We both explained to the deputy that we play up here all the time and this was the first time we had ever had a problem.

"Is the sheriff going to be okay?" Dora asked, with deep concern in her voice.

Deputy John looked at Dora with tears in his eyes.

"I don't know Dora, he's hurt awful bad. The bear really did a job on him. We found him way up the hill in that big trap that Old Mad Jack had made for the grizzly bear. It looked like he had made his way to the edge of the trap and fell in, all the way to the bottom. He had to have hit hard because the trap is over thirty feet deep. I think the trap is the only thing that saved him from the bear. The grizzly must have been afraid to jump in the hole."

"We saw bear sign all around the edge of the big hole where he had been circling. That grizzly must have spent hours trying to figure out how to get to the sheriff."

"As we were busy getting Sheriff Mike out of the hole, we heard the grizzly making his way back. We had to lower Sheriff Mike back into the hole, to keep him safe. With a bear that size, we could not take a chance of not being able to stop him, and we wanted Sheriff Mike to be out of harms way."

"As the grizzly got closer to us, we could hear him grunting and groaning like he was still really mad. I don't think he had one happy bone in his old hide."

"Before the grizzly came within sight, we all started looking for a tree to climb. Joe and Tom were able to climb into the trees before the grizzly saw them. Dave and I weren't so lucky. Before we got up the tree, the grizzly came into view. He saw us and charged on all fours."

"I had been closer to him than Dave was, so he came after me first. I was able to make it to the other side of the big hole that Mad Jack had dug.

I pulled my pistol out of its holster, but in my haste it slipped out of my hand and fell into the hole."

"The grizzly was coming directly at me, and had not seen the hole between us. He stopped short of going over the edge, almost falling down where the sheriff was."

"He did not seem to appreciate the hole between us and started around the edge after me. I ran in the opposite direction. He noticed that I was running the opposite way, turned around came right at me. I turned, running away from him again."

"The grizzly saw this, turned and started running toward me again. This happened three or four times and would have been downright funny if it had not been such a grave life and death situation."

"As the bear and I were playing tag, Dave had been able to find a tree to climb. The bear was all mine, or maybe the other way around."

"I was getting tired, but I noticed the grizzly was slowing down also. Or at least I thought he was."

"Everything was happening so fast that the other deputies were afraid to shoot. They were concerned the bullet might hit me. They were yelling and waving their arms, trying to get his attention. It appeared that he was more interested in playing with me then he was playing games with them.

He let out another tremendous roar and started a new attack at me."

"He was moving faster then before. His mouth was wide open and fangs at least three inches long were exposed. I was very impressed. I took off as fast as I could. He had got so close to me, at this point, it was no longer a game. He was less then six feet from me."

"I knew that I was dead he might get me at any moment. I started praying out loud. *Lord, please help me*. At that exact moment my foot hit a soft spot on the edge of the hole and down I went."

"I hit hard, just missing Sheriff Mike. All the air was knocked completely out of me, and my leg hurt like blazes. I could hear the grizzly having a temper tantrum above me."

"He had his big head over the edge of the hole, making all kinds of menacing sounds. I was glad I was down here. And hoping the big grizzly would not jump in the hole after me. The big Grizzly reared up on his hind legs and let out a vicious growl. It was so loud and ferocious it seemed to shake the whole forest. It looked like he had decided not to jump in the hole. *Thank you Lord*."

"Dave, seeing me fall down the hole, immediately started shooting. At that point I could hear all the deputies shooting at the grizzly bear. He was screaming in pure rage. He then took off into the dense brush and all was quite."

"I silently laid in the hole, listening for any sounds from above. It must have been at least ten minutes before I heard the deputies again."

"Then Dave stuck his head over the edge and yelled. 'Are you okay John?' I told him I was fine except my leg was hurt. They got the sheriff and me out of the hole as fast as they could and we started down the trail."

"We had gone only about fifty feet when all of a sudden the grizzly was in front of us again. He stood up on his hind legs, let out a big bellow, then fell flat on his face. He was dead."

As Deputy John finished his story, Dora and I had been walking down the trail with them, I had not noticed, but it was starting to cloud up real bad. When it rained up here, it could be a real cloud-burst. We decided we had better go on down with the deputy and come back tomorrow.

A movement from the stretcher caught my eye. The sheriff had come to.

He saw us immediately and tried to rise up, but could not. He kind of waved at me with his good hand and then went back to sleep. It looked like sheriff Mike was going to be okay. *"Thank you Lord for holding the sheriff in your loving hands."*

CHAPTER 23

The Return of the Black Demon

It was late afternoon before we got back to the house. Sheriff Mike was in a lot of pain and Deputy John's leg was giving him problems also. Momma saw us coming and ran out the door to see if she could help. Deputy John said no, as they had to get back to town as soon as possible, and get the sheriff some medical attention. Momma saw how bad the deputy was limping and told him that she insisted they come into the house.

The deputy finally agreed to accept my moms help. When they were comfortable, momma put on a pot of coffee and took some hot rolls out of the oven.

The sheriff had woke up by now and appeared to be doing okay. He told momma that he was still hurting real bad in his right side and his back. Momma brought out some kind of ointment and applied to the sheriffs' back and side. She told him that this would make him feel a lot better.

Seeing the deputy was hurting, she also applied some of the ointment to his leg.

I noticed the coffee was done perking so I washed my hands and got out cups for everybody. Momma had set the hot rolls on the table so I got saucers from the cupboard and gave everyone a roll. Bless their hearts. I think they were all starved as they downed the rolls almost in one bite. Even the sheriffs' roll disappeared, as if by magic.

Momma noticed this also and rushed back into the kitchen. She returned in just a few minutes with big bowls of steaming hot hobo stew and some more rolls.

The sheriff saw what momma had brought into the living room and almost sat up straight. He let out a big groan and fell back down on the stretcher. Bless his heart, I thought, he better be more careful.

After everybody was full and feeling better, momma finally sat down with us.

The sheriff asked momma what she had put on his back and side. He told her that the pain was almost all gone and that he felt really good.

Deputy John also mentioned that his pain was completely gone. "I would like to know also. That stuff works miracles."

Momma told them that the lotion was an old recipe that her mother had shown her when she was a child. It was just a mixture of pine tree sap, morel mushrooms ground up, cayenne pepper, and a little mustard mixed with ground up garlic.

The most important ingredient though was sheep sorrel. Sheep sorrel grows wild in the mountains. The mixture has to be just right with the proper amount of ingredients for it to work properly.

She said her mother had learned it from her grandmother, and that an old Cherokee lady had taught her. The recipe for the ointment came from a long way back.

Dora and I had been eating also and just listening to the conversation the deputies and sheriff were having about what they had experienced up on Grouse Mountain.

The time had really flown, by now, and it was almost nine p.m. Momma told the sheriff and deputies that she would feel better if they would stay the night and get an early start in the morning. Libby was about twenty five miles away and it was still pouring down rain.

Dora, hearing what momma had said about the time, all of a sudden jumped out of her chair. 'Oh my!" she exclaimed, as she ran out the door, "I've got to get home. My mom told me I had to be home by nine at the latest. Bye everybody."

Deputy John looked at the sheriff and saw that he was comfortable and maybe it would be better if they waited until morning.

Next morning the rain had stopped and I woke up about seven o'clock.

Momma had got up real early and had already fed everybody. The sheriff and deputies were all gone. I felt bad I had not been able to tell them goodbye. Momma said the sheriff had told her that he would be in touch with me, because there were a lot of questions that still had to be answered. This made me feel better, as I had grown a fondness for all of them.

I went out to do my chores and found Dora at the barn waiting for me. Bless her heart, she had already milked three of the goats for me and then staked them out. She was starting to milk the fourth one. What a friend she was. I think I love her. Of course I just thought this and would not say it out loud. She might think I was being silly or something.

As we finished all my chores and had started back to the house with the milk, I noticed something black behind one of the bushes. Thinking it might just be one of the old barn cats, I disregarded it and kept walking.

As I passed the bush, all of a sudden it looked like the bush exploded. You guessed it. This big black round ball of fur with fangs as long as telephone poles came hurdling toward me. It scared me so bad; I dropped both pails on the ground, spilling all the milk.

"Jerry, Jerry, get off Lester. Look what you've done. You made Lester spill all the milk on the ground. Bad, Jerry. Go home. Go home now."

Boy, Dora was really mad at Jerry. I have never seen her so mad. She picked up a big stick and started chasing Jerry with it. He knew he was in trouble big time. He put his tail between his legs and it looked like he had taken off for home.

We had a hard time explaining to my mom why I had spilled the milk. She knew about the black demon, disguised as playful little dog, and decided it probably wasn't my fault. She said I needed to be more careful next time and not to play with Jerry when I was doing my chores.

I asked momma if we could go back up on Copper and she said we could. We took off on a run. Dora again was in the lead. When she heard momma say okay, she had taken off like a shot.

CHAPTER 24

GeeGee and BeeBee
Go Home

I grabbed a few things I thought we might need and we started up the old trail heading to Copper Mountain. Considering the heavy rain yesterday, it was pretty nice out. The sun was just coming over the mountain and it was starting to get warm.

I looked around for Bozo. He had heard Dora yelling at Jerry and took off for the forest. I really wanted him to go with us up the mountain. He was very good about letting us know if danger was ahead. Besides that the way he was always barking most animals stayed clear of us.

I could not see him anywhere so I started after Dora. She had looked back at me several times. I think she was wondering why I wasn't right behind her.

I called a few more times, but Bozo did not come. I figured if he wanted to go with us he could catch up later. I took off after Dora.

She was quite a ways ahead of me by now. I think she wanted to get to the mine before me.

We were about halfway up to the old mine when I heard some loud noises over the edge of the hill. We quietly made our way to look over the edge.

Way down below us was a big bear standing over a large deer. It looked like he had just put it down and was going to have it for his lunch.

We were far enough from the big bear that he did not know we were there. It looked like he would be busy for a long time so we were not afraid and continued up the mountain.

As we approached the old mine we noticed the ore car that had been sitting on top of the tailing pile was gone. I didn't think anything about it, but I did wonder why it wasn't there.

Just then GeeGee appeared in the mine opening. BeeBee was right behind her. There were several large eagles circling overhead, as if they were watching for any danger. I thought to myself, how nice it was that the Lord had supplied flying guardians for the Hgiahs. Bozo was with them also.

I hadn't seen Bozo for a couple hours, since we had left the house and had wondered where he was. Now here he is with GeeGee and BeeBee. He must have known where we were headed and beat us here.

GeeGee again motioned for us to follow her. She seemed to have an impatient attitude about her and I was wondering why. From what I had learned of her, she pretty much was always in control of her emotions, except when we found BeeBee.

As we proceeded back into the old mine shaft my crystal again started to vibrate, except this time there was a very beautiful harmonious hum accompanying the vibration. It seemed like the entire walls of the mine were vibrating at the same frequency as my crystal.

The gold pieces, that Dora and I had noticed several days before in the walls of the mine, were shining with a very beautiful radiant gold light that seemed to envelope my entire being. The light emanating from them was penetrating everything in the tunnel, including us. The radiance was stunning. I had never seen any thing quite like this.

The vibration appeared to be upsetting Bozo and he took off for the entrance. I let him go, figuring he could find his way home, if need be.

As we walked, or I think maybe we were just floating along, the hum changed frequency and the vibration from my crystal sped up. As this happened, GeeGee pulled her amulet out and started pressing several of the symbols on the back.

Things started happening fast. We were now in the large cavern where the tiny mounds were. "Wow this is really beautiful!" I exclaimed. Before I could utter another word, I was compelled to hand my crystal over to GeeGee. No words had been spoken I just knew what to do.

GeeGee took the crystal and held it in her left hand. With her right hand she reached out toward BeeBee. BeeBee grabbed her hand and they stood there in the cavern, silently. No words were spoken and there was an absolute silence filling the air. Stillness was everywhere. Nothing was moving.

All the walls of the cavern lit up as if by the hand of God himself. I could feel Gods love as I have never experienced in my whole life. Not even in the land of Hgiah was the feeling of love this strong.

As the feeling of God's all mighty love filled the air, I heard angels singing. The music was coming from every corner of the cavern.

I felt like I was actually in heaven. What a feeling. As the experience of peace and tranquility was flowing over my entire body, GeeGee motioned for Dora and myself to hold hands with them. We formed a circle and GeeGee placed my crystal right in the center. The crystal started glowing brightly and a holograph of Jocko appeared.

Jocko raised his hands and turned facing GeeGee. I could feel his words rather then hear them. They seemed to be in a foreign language.

I glanced over at GeeGee and she appeared to be understanding what jocko was saying. After about five minutes the holograph disappeared.

GeeGee reached down and picked up the crystal and handed it to me. She asked Dora and BeeBee to bring their amulets forth. As she did so she walked over toward the mounds.

As we approached the mounds, the jewels on top of each one started glowing. A ray of red light shot from each one of the jewels. The rays culminated in a single apex, about a foot above the tops of the mounds.

GeeGee reached out with her hand and the Creationism Stone appeared. She placed the stone on the very spot where the rays of light came together. She then motioned for us to follow her.

GeeGee stopped about ten feet from the mounds and placed her amulet on a round flat rock. BeeBee placed her amulet next to GeeGee's, about a foot away. GeeGee then motioned for Dora to place Jonus's amulet next to the others. As she did so the amulets moved to where they formed a perfect triangle.

As I was watching, it seems I knew exactly what to do. I walked over to where the amulets were and placed my crystal right in the center of the triangle. As I did so a steady hum started permeating the cavern. GeeGee motioned for us all to stand back and hold hands and we formed a perfect circle around the amulets. As we did so the hum turned into a deep vibrating crescendo.

The entire cavern was as if it was alive. Everything was moving and we were moving with it. I heard beautiful music. It seemed to be coming from all around me. Then I felt like I was dreaming and floating on a cloud. I was oblivious to all my surroundings, as if I was in a deep sleep.

CHAPTER 25

Back to the Land of Hgiah

The next moment I will never forget. We were standing in a beautiful valley. The rolling hills had a bluish sheen about them, with beautiful rays of light emanating into the valley. The light rays extended clear across the open meadow, as if giving the valley a protective shield of some sort. I totally expected angels to be gliding along the rays of light.

There were animals of all kinds. Deer, elk, lions, sheep, tigers, elephants, panthers, well, every animal I have ever heard about, all grazing peacefully together. Indeed, it was a paradise.

There was soft music, as if angels were singing, coming from all around. The peace and tranquility that I felt, reminded me of when Dora and I were exiting the cavern, after we fell into the whirlpool, when we were lost in Canada. Again it reminded me of the Garden of Eden.

I was totally lost in the moment, enjoying the absolute beauty that was surrounding me, and did not notice the cloud materializing on the beautiful carpet of grass in front of me.

Only when the music ceased, did I become aware of the clouds presence. Oh my, I couldn't believe my eyes. The cloud was floating about one foot above the ground. The colors had the appearance of a very bright rainbow. There were two figures standing in the very center of the cloud.

As the cloud floated closer to us we were able to make out who the figures were. It was Jocko and Oohma.

Dora had noticed Jocko and Oohma at the same moment as I, and she started running toward them. Oohma reached out and Dora jumped right into her arms. She wrapped her arms around Oohma. Oohma gave Dora a huge hug and then gently placed her on the ground.

GeeGee and BeeBee were not too far behind Dora.

All of a sudden, Asheena, Madeena and Ladeena, appeared out of nowhere. There were two tall Hgiahs with them that I had never seen before.

They all stopped short as they saw each other. They all started crying and wrapped their arms around each other. After a short while GeeGee came over toward Dora and me. She had big tears of joy in her eyes as she took our hands. "Come," she said. "I want you to meet our fathers. My fathers' name is Enocha, and BeeBees father is Setha."

Asheena, watching the reunion, and waiting until all the crying had stopped, came over and said. "Lester, you and Dora have done something we Hgiahs could not do. We tried everything we could think of to rescue GeeGee and BeeBee, but we could not find them. This is nothing short of a miracle, that you were able to find rescue them."

No sooner had Asheena said this, Enocha grabbed me and Setha grabbed Dora. They threw us in the air and onto their shoulders.

Jocko then came toward us with a big smile on his face. As he passed Asheena, he grabbed her hand, and they stopped in front of us.

"This is a glorious day. You have brought our lost children safely back to us. For this wonderful moment we need to celebrate. But first we must prepare. Our reunion with the Ancient of Days is this afternoon."

"You both are invited to participate in this most sacred occasion."

Jocko then glanced at Enocha and Setha and they both nodded their heads. They took us into a large temple where the walls were as shimmering waterfalls. In the middle of the large round room was a round pool above the floor about three feet deep. There was a ledge on the pool about a foot wide. The surface of the ledge looked like mother of pearl. The side of the pool looked as if it was made from pure silver. Every foot or so was a vertical line about two inches wide that looked like diamonds. The diamonds had a beautiful glow about them lighting up the entire room.

They placed Both Dora and myself in the pool. There was no water, even though it looked like water. I felt a high frequency vibration like my entire body and soul were being cleansed.

The next thing I knew Dora and I were in a beautiful room with flowers everywhere. The fragrance was wonderful and soothing.

Just then Dora grabbed my arm. "Lester, look at our clothes!"

"We have on beautiful outfits just like Jocko and Asheena."

"Wow these are really great!" I exclaimed. Just then, Jocko, Asheena, GeeGee and BeeBee appeared.

A big tray of food was on a table in the middle of the room. Somehow I had not noticed it before. It was like it came from out of nowhere.

Jocko extended his big hands and we all stood in a circle holding hands as Jocko prayed.

"Thank you All Mighty One for the safe return of our children. And we thank you for Lester and Dora, for without them this day may never have come to pass. We ask you now to spread your gracious love on us as we celebrate and get ready for our reunion with you. Place us in your protection and keep us on your path as we continue our preparations. Thank You All Mighty One, Amen."

All the Hgiahs waited until Oohma had set down. Then Jocko sat at the right of Oohma and Asheena sat at her left. Jocko then motioned for me to sit next to him and Dora to sit next to Asheena. After we had taken our seats, and only then, did the other Hgiahs sit down.

I was totally awed at the respect and love that was shown toward Oohma.

As we finished eating, as if by some divine hand, we were back in the luscious green pasture. GeeGee and BeeBee both knelt down on their knees in front of their parents. Jocko and Asheena also knelt down. They all formed a circle, holding hands. Oohma was in the middle. All the other Hgiahs had formed a circle around them. They were all looking into the sky.

I looked up also and was astounded at what was materializing above us. A ring of soft pink fluffy clouds encircled the area where we were standing. Shining from the clouds were rays of pink light, which were forming a circle all the way around us. The rays extended all the way from the cloud to the ground. Clear blue sky was visible straight above us. All was still with no movement anywhere. There was complete calmness with no sound.

As I was standing there in absolute wonder as to what was happening, a large orb of light appeared right in the center of the cloud circle.

The sound of beautiful music was all around us. I felt in my heart that angels were singing once again.

Jocko, Asheena, Ladeena, Madeena, GeeGee, BeeBee and Oohma had stood up and were slowly backing up, forming a huge circle in front of them. Jocko motioned for Dora and me to join their circle and we all held hands. As we did so a beautiful ray of blue light was projected from the orb. The ray of light extended to the ground right in the center of our huge circle.

As we all watched in silence, I noticed that something was forming on the ground in front of us. The object was round and flat like a disk. The shape of the disk reminded me of a large silver dollar, or maybe a huge amulet. Yes, that's what it is. It's a huge amulet. Wow the surface looked just like Uncle Jonus's amulet. I could even see symbols appearing on the surface of the disk. Each symbol was surrounded with a circle.

Jocko noticed the questionable look on my face and smiled. He then explained that the symbols represented each Hgiah, and the disk was called the "Wheel of Life". Every living Hgiah on or in earth is represented here.

The disk just kept growing. It must have been at least a thousand feet across. The light from the orb was lighting the whole surface of the disk.

I was so absorbed in what was happening in front of me that I did not notice a crowd forming. There must have been a thousand or more Hgiahs standing around the perimeter of the disk.

Oohma had started walking forward and then suddenly appeared in the center of the disk next to a round pedestal about three feet high, as if she had been teleported. Oohma then turned toward Jocko and made a wide sweeping gesture.

I was deep in thought, enjoying the extreme beauty of the scene before me, when Jocko gently took my hand in his huge hand and started walking forward. I noticed Asheena had taken Dora's hand also and they were following Jocko and me.

As we approached the disk, stairs formed in front of us, and we stepped up and walked toward Oohma. Oohma was standing directly over a very beautiful ornate symbol next to the round pedestal.

On the very top of the pedestal was another representation of an amulet. This amulet was different than any I had ever seen.

It looked like it was made from pure gold. It was very beautiful

Jocko stopped right next to Oohma and stepped on another symbol. As he did so, all the symbols, on the surface of the disk lit up with a beautiful blue glow. He then raised his hands toward the orb.

As he did this Asheena and Dora came forward and stood right next to Jocko and me. Asheena also stood on another symbol. She then motioned for Dora and myself to stand next to them. Each of us was directed to stand in an empty circle. She then raised her hands toward the orb.

All the Hgiahs that had been standing around the edge, now moved forward and climbed aboard the disk. Each one moved to a circle and stood on their respective symbol.

As the last Hgiah took their place, they all held hands. We were right between Jocko and Asheena.

As I looked around it appeared that every symbol on the disk was occupied save one. I was about to question Jocko about the empty symbol when a strong vibrational hum filled the air. I could feel a strong vibration coming from somewhere beneath my feet. Dora looked up at Asheena with deep concern in her eyes. Asheena had seen this and telepathically told us not to worry. She continued saying we were about to experience something no human had ever experienced before us. We were about to meet the Ancient of Days.

No sooner had Asheena said this, the disk started rising off the ground. The high frequency hum, that was enveloping the entire platform, seemed to form a force field of some sort over the disk. It looked like we were on our way.

The disk levitated into the sky. It seemed like we more than a thousand feet off the ground, when all of sudden it took off like a rocket ship. There was no sensation of flying, but I knew we were. Darkness enveloped us and I could see stars all around. I think we were headed out into space.

Looking around, I noticed all the Hgiahs were holding their amulets with their left hand. They had their right hand extended upward.

The deep vibration, that was enveloping the entire area within the dome, was getting louder. The frequency of the vibration was very soothing. It felt wonderful.

I just knew that whatever was ahead of us would be the biggest most exciting and wonderful thing that has ever happened to any human. I felt truly blessed.

I believe in my heart of hearts, we were about to find out, "From Whence They Came."

Printed in the United States
by Baker & Taylor Publisher Services